Linnet

Linnet

SALLY WATSON

E. P. Dutton & Co., Inc.   New York

Published simultaneously in Canada by Clarke,
Irwin & Company Limited, Toronto and Vancouver

SBN: 0–525–33695–8   LCC: 76–157952

Designed by Dorothea von Elbe
Printed in the U.S.A.
First Edition

———•—

For
Ivy and Len
true Londoners and dearest of friends

Contents

1

The Road to London

She was an elf of a girl, with the face of a freckled pixie and a most impish gleam dwelling in greenish eyes. But the gleam wasn't much in evidence at the moment. She sat on a high grassy bank by the Portsmouth-to-London road nursing a blistered heel and looking forlorn and a little scared.

The rider, his servants behind him, pulled his horse to a stop and stared down at her speculatively. Not a waif or gypsy, after all, he realized almost at once. For her fine woollen cloak was lined with sky-blue silk, and from beneath it peeped a snowy lace ruff and shoes of blue leather. Moreover, the soft rosy-brown of the cloak had been chosen with love and artistry as a foil for her wealth of red hair. For even young girls these days were dying their hair red in loving imitation of their glorious Queen Bess. . . .

He looked closer, as the hood of the cloak fell back from the tilted head. No! That hair had never been dyed. It was the apricot-red of polished copper, and a long strand of it blew loose across a splatter of matching freckles. The freckles in turn adorned a saucy small face that looked up at him with a mixture of anxiety and truculence—with a pointed chin, a wide mouth, and a pair of eyebrows that were a dead giveaway to her character, had the rider but known it. The one behaved beautifully, following the bone in a pure curve like a gull's wing. The other, erratic and willful as its owner, stopped in mid-curve, and shot a long and altogether unexpected arrow of hairs outward at a rakish angle. It almost distracted the rider's attention from the fact that the dark spiky lashes showed traces of damp.

This was a most unlikely place to find a young girl of the gentry or perhaps even nobility! Even in this modern and civilized year of 1582, a highway was not precisely safe.

"My dear child!" exclaimed the rider. "Whatever are you doing here, and alone? May I help?"

She studied him cautiously. Mother had taught her never to speak to strangers, and Giles had remarked quite recently and rudely that she was a gullible little goose. But this was just the insulting sort of remark Giles was always making, and now that she was out in the world, Linnet proposed to show just how shrewd and sagacious she could be.

The rider was a fine young man on a good horse, attended by two strapping servants who looked capable of dealing with any number of highwaymen. His pointed beard was impeccably trimmed, his hose and doublet and short fashionable cloak were made of the finest cloth and cut, his ruff was enormous, his gloves were embroidered, he had three long feathers in his cap; he could not conceivably be a gypsy or vagrant or highwayman. She decided to trust him.

"I'm having an adventure," she confided. "Only 'tis not turning out precisely as I'd intended, because of the blisters on my heel, and London being just a trifle farther from Guildford than I'd thought it to be. And," she added with a small sigh, "I am hungry."

He failed to notice this hint, but sat regarding her with an expression of quizzical amusement. "I feel quite certain your family can't approve of this adventure," he decided. "Are you a runaway, my poppet?"

She drew herself up with what she hoped was simply shattering dignity. "I'm not your poppet," she informed him. "I'm not anyone's poppet. I'll have you know I'm fourteen."

"I do beg your pardon, Milady!" he exclaimed at once in the most gratifying manner, and swept his plumed hat from his head. "I should have seen at once that you're not a child."

"Yes, you should," Linnet agreed with great severity. But then, seeing that his lip was quivering with emotion at this reproof, she relented. "My family do the same thing, and they *know* how old I am," she conceded, frowning at the memory. "They've never taken me to see the Queen, for instance; they say I'm too irresponsible and would be sure to say the wrong things or be rude to the French and Spanish ambassadors—" She paused, considering this. "Well, I probably would, too, and I don't see why I shouldn't, the way they keep plotting with that horrid Mary of Scotland to murder our Queen and turn England over to the Pope!" She scowled ferociously. "And Giles says there are still a lot of *English* Papists ready to help put Mary on the throne, even after all those other plots failed, the traitors! I wish I could help save the Queen from them, don't you?"

3

He looked fascinated. "What did you have in mind, exactly?"

Linnet frowned. "Well, I don't know yet. How could I, stuck way out in the middle of Wiltshire?"

"Wiltshire?" The rider looked confused, as well he might. The Portsmouth road didn't go within two counties of Wiltshire, which was far to the west. Linnet didn't notice the confusion, for she was fixing him with a hopeful eye. He looked quite wealthy enough to treat a young lady to dinner.

"I don't suppose you have any food in your saddlebag?" she suggested delicately. "I'm most heartily famished. I did mention it once before, you know, and I think you ought to have taken the hint."

" 'Twas most remiss of me," he confessed at once. "The fact is, I'm so fascinated by you, I've forgot my manners." He gestured to the less massive of his two servants, who began fishing in the saddlebag. "Tell me, Mistress, would it sound too much like a bribe if I were to offer you food in exchange for hearing all about you?"

She giggled. "Well, if you put it that way, it certainly would. Why don't you just say, 'My food is yours, fair lady, and whilst you eat I would fain hear thy story'? Only first I think you had better introduce yourself, so I won't be talking to a strange man, which I'm not allowed to do, you know." She looked up at him expectantly.

He at once took his foot from the bank where it had been propped, and made a deep bow, with flourishes.

"Sir Colin Collyngewood of Collyngewood Hall, at your service, Milady," he said grandly.

Linnet leaped to her feet and curtseyed, wincing as the

blistered heels protested. "And I'm Mistress Linnet Seymour of Fontenay, and give you good den, Sir Colin, so now everything's quite proper, isn't it?"

But he shook his head at her, frowning. "My dear young lady, you are *far* too trusting! How do you know that's my real name? How do you know I'm not a liar and the greatest rogue in Christendom?"

The less massive servant, in the act of handing his master a parcel wrapped in a napkin looked startled. Linnet stared, a trifle shaken just for a moment. "Well, you don't *look* like a rogue," she said uncertainly. "Or sound like one, either."

"Certainly not. 'Tis a rogue's business not to. I could be six kinds of knave, for all that." And he frowned at her with the air of a stoat eyeing a rabbit.

She stared back, entranced. "What six kinds?" she demanded.

The larger servant choked slightly. Sir Colin blinked once and then began counting on his fingers. "Kidnapper," he suggested ominously. "Murderer. Highwayman. Coney-catcher. Forger. Horse-thief. I might be engaged in selling state secrets and then blackmailing the men who told them to me. And," he added for good measure, "I might run a kynchin school, for training cutpurses, pickpockets, burglars, and ambush thieves." And with another bow he politely handed Linnet the packet of food.

"Cold goose and white bread!" said Linnet happily. She bit. Then she waved a wing at him and talked around her mouthful. "If you were all those things, or even just one or two of them, you wouldn't tell me about it," she pointed out, and bit again. She was very hungry. "This is delicious

5

goose, Sir Colin, and I'm very much obliged to you," she added politely.

"My pleasure." He twinkled at her. "And if I were all those things, I might tell you so just to disarm your suspicions."

Linnet chuckled. "I almost wish you were," she told him, eyes dancing. "It would be so very interesting to meet someone like that, and learn all about it, and have some adventures, and then go back and tell Giles. That would show him! He always thinks he knows everything." She bit into the goose again, as though it were Giles.

Sir Colin rested his booted foot on the grassy bank again and flicked his riding whip through his fingers. "And who is Giles?" he inquired with friendly interest.

"Oh, he's sort of an unrelated god-brother. That is, his parents are my godparents, and my parents are his godparents, so he thinks that gives him the right to make insulting remarks. One would think he really was one of my family. They all treat me like the veriest babe, and a simpleminded babe at that, just because I happen to be the youngest."

Sir Colin was looking very sympathetic. "Welladay! That's hardly your fault, is it? What sort of things do they say?"

"Well, just because I'm not intellectual, they call me things like Twitterwit and Featherhead, and then pretend it's just because I was named after a bird." Sir Colin looked inquiring. "Linnet, you know. You see, Mother was a famous Greek scholar, so they named their first daughters Penelope and Phoebe; and then they named Gil and Cecily from the family tree; and then they thought it would be nice to have another boy named Robert, only he turned out to be me. So Father said they'd better have another bird because Mother's named Robin, so they named me Linnet. Actually, they gave me two other names as well, one from the Greeks and one from the family tree, but I shall never tell anyone what they are!" She looked outraged. "And they treat me as if I'm bird-witted besides!"

He was looking at her sardonically. "And so you've run off to London to prove them wrong?"

Linnet fixed him with a displeased stare. "You're beginning to sound just like Mother," she told him coldly. "And if anyone is more exasperating than Giles and Father, 'tis Mother."

"Are they so strict, then?" He was looking surprised. He somehow hadn't got that impression.

Linnet shook her coppery head. "Worse than that," she sighed. "They're reasonable." He didn't look as if he fully comprehended the awfulness of this, so she undertook to explain. "Don't you see? If they were strict, I could argue back, or rebel, or something, and feel that I was right. But when they're reasonable, all they do is expect me to be reasonable too, and if I'm not—I mean, if—" He had begun to laugh silently. She looked at him. "Yes, you see how frustrating it is? I mean, how can you fight something like that?"

"You can run away from home, I gather," he suggested, settling himself down on the grassy bank not too near a patch of stinging nettles with an air of being infinitely entertained and quite willing to stop all day, and not even caring if his fine mauve hose and yellow trunks were stained or not. The servants crossed the road to tether the horses and settle themselves in the shade, with a patient

7

"what now?" air that Linnet thought rather impudent for fellows of their station. The lower orders should always be treated kindly, of course, but they ought also to be well trained.

"Well, you're wrong," she told Sir Colin. "I haven't run away from home at all. How could I? I did try once, but they just said to be sure to take plenty of food and old Jemmy to guard me, and hadn't I best take a feather pillow as it's quite uncomfortable sleeping on the road. So of course I started laughing, and everything was quite spoiled."

Sir Colin was looking unaccountably puzzled. "But— you're here," he pointed out with an air of grasping at what he hoped was solid fact.

"Yes, but I haven't run away from *home*," Linnet explained. "I wouldn't be on this road if I had, because home's in Wiltshire. I've run away from Giles and my godparents, but they don't know it." The gentleman wasn't looking greatly enlightened, so she offered him a bit of his own goose to encourage mental activity, took another herself, and explained further. She was quite enjoying this. She had never had a better audience. And she had been, to tell the truth, feeling very lonely.

"You see, every summer Giles comes to Fontenay or I go to his house, and this year it's my turn there. And they aren't particularly reasonable at all, but only quite normal, except for Giles, of course, who is *just* like Mother. But I'm not speaking to him just now, anyway. So it was quite possible to run away from there, and I did it very cleverly, too, so no one will worry. They think I'm on my way home with Sir Guy after my visit, and my family thinks I'm still in Guildford."

She smiled at Sir Colin, awaiting his admiration. It came. "That's very clever indeed!" he said warmly. "But just what were you planning to do next?"

She sighed and regarded her aching feet, suddenly not quite as sanguine as she had been. "Well, when I get to London I can go to Hertford House and make myself known to my Cousin Edward, and perhaps he'll invite me to stay for his wedding, and—"

"Hertford!" He stared. "Satan's teeth, you little minx, are you one of *those* Seymours?"

Linnet regarded him with severity. "Well, I don't think you ought to call me a minx," she complained. "It isn't really at *all* a compliment, you know. *I* can't help it if my Seymour great-uncles went around beheading each other and everyone after King Hal died; and anyway, it was only those two, and not my grandfather at all. *He* stayed in Wiltshire. And Father and Mother left Court before the nasty bit happened, too, and they've never seen any of that branch of Seymours since. They never liked them, anyway." She sighed. "That is one thing that worries me just a tiny bit," she confessed. "When I just show up, without so much as a warning or a letter or anything, do you think — Well, do you think they might take it amiss?" She pushed her hood further back on her shoulders and looked rather anxiously at her new friend, who was pulling on his pointed beard and looking a trifle odd.

"My dear Mistress Seymour!" he said. "How very fortunate that I came by! Have you any notion how far it still is to London? 'Tis over thirty miles; I doubt you've come more than six or eight. Moreover, you are quite right not to want to arrive at your cousins' unannounced, much less dusty and on foot. I think you'd never get past the first footman. No, you had best come with me."

"I don't think I had best do that at all," retorted Linnet, turning prim. "Mother wouldn't approve."

"She wouldn't approve your being here to begin with," he reminded her unanswerably. "Nor would she approve your spending the night beside the road."

He had a strong argument. Linnet considered it, along with the prospect of seeing him and his stalwart servants riding on and leaving her here alone. She decided to compromise.

"I'll ride with you to London," she agreed, "and then you can just let me off at my Cousin Edward's house." She smiled engagingly, producing a tiny dimple just at the corner of her mouth and causing her wayward eyebrow to twitch. "I'm very much obliged to you, and I've eaten most of your bread and goose, but would you like what's left?"

Linnet undertook to entertain her benefactor the rest of the way to London. For one thing, it seemed only polite to offer him amusement in return for food and escort, and for another, he was a splendid listener. He seemed genuinely interested in everything: her home, her family, her likes and dislikes and opinions. To be sure, he did tend to laugh now and then when Linnet wasn't being funny, and just once he gave her a wondering look.

"My dear young lady, did anyone ever tell you that you talk too much?"

"Frequently," returned Linnet just a trifle tartly. "So I hope you're not going to. As a matter of fact, Mother keeps telling me in the most annoyingly reasonable way that God gave me two ears and only one tongue, so He must mean me to listen twice as much as I talk. But I don't at all agree with that. I think He just gave me two ears so I can hear in two directions. Besides, since He gave me a nature that likes to talk, I should think He means me to."

"You may have a point," agreed Sir Colin. "Then you don't much take after your mother?"

"Well, I'm not as brilliant or even as reasonable, but then none of us are. Penelope comes closest to that, but 'tis Cecy who looks like Mother, and so does her little baby Rob. I just have her nose and chin and teeth; and my freckles and this silly eyebrow are from Father; and so is my hair. Father's reasonable, too, by the way. Did I mention that? I think Gil's the least reasonable of all of us, and he's a self-righteous prig besides, and I am glad I'm not Frances! That's his wife. Being married to Gil would be even worse than being married to Giles, and that would be bad enough, but at least Giles has a sense of humor, and he enjoys life, and to tell you the truth, I think he's a lot more reckless underneath than he pretends. He thinks he has to be stuffy to be a good example to me."

Frowning slightly, she fell into profound thought— for at least two minutes.

2

Hospitality

Linnet, raised in the tranquility of the Wiltshire countryside of softly curving emerald hills and graceful woods,
was astounded by London. Tall narrow houses, each story
jutting out farther than the one below, staggered drunk-
enly along the road, built against one another but by no
means in a straight line. Linnet's eyes became rounder and
rounder, and at last she turned to peer up at the new friend
who was so kindly sharing his horse with her.

"Marry, I'd never thought London was so big!" she
marveled.

He laughed. "My dear child, we're not in London yet.
This is called Southwark. You can see the playhouses and
bear pit up ahead. But we won't be in London until we've
crossed the Thames."

Linnet fell into an awed silence, thankful that she was
not, after all, on foot and alone.

It was the hyacinth-colored dusk of May when they finally reached London Bridge, so built with houses and shops
that it didn't seem a bridge at all, but only, disappoint-
ingly, another street. And then they were in London
Town. Linnet looked around the thronged streets, swallowed hard, and spoke around a lump. She wasn't afraid, of

course; it was just that a lump happened to be there.

"Thank you very much for the ride, Sir Colin, and now I must go find my cousins." And she moved to slip down from the horse—but not very urgently. It was a relief to feel his lean strong hand preventing it.

"Not so fast there, my dear. Have you the least idea where your cousins live? Or whether they are actually in London just now at all?"

Linnet blinked in the dusk. She started to say yes. Then she started to say that she could just ask someone. Then she looked around at the gathering dark. Torches began to flare here and there where a man-at-arms led his master through the narrow and somehow menacing streets. The gutters down the center stank, and people lurked in the shadows and corners in a most unnerving way. She changed her mind about asking any of them and shook her hooded head forlornly. But then the comforting solidness of Sir Colin cheered her up.

"You'll find it for me, won't you?"

"Not tonight," he said firmly. "Quite out of the question, my dear. You had best come along home with me and get something to eat, and we'll decide then what's to be done." And the horse moved on before Linnet could decide whether or not to agree.

Not that she had much choice, really. The streets were distinctly unsavory, not nearly as glamorous as she had supposed London to be. But presently they came to a slightly better district, and then crossed the huge width of Chepeside Street, and presently stopped before a fine tall house with a wall in front.

"My home," said Sir Colin. "I call it Over House."

"Why?" asked Linnet, curious. "I mean, if it's over, then what's under? There are towns in Hampshire, you know, named Over Wallop, and Nether Wallop, and Middle Wa—" She stopped, eyeing the servants suspiciously. She was sure one of them had chortled, and she had not intended to be funny. "Why do you call it that?" she repeated with dignity.

"I just do," said Sir Colin, shrugging. "Now, you must be hungry again. Will you come in and let Kitty bring hot water to wash, and then honor me by supping with me?"

Linnet thought briefly of all the things Mother had told her.

Then she thought of a hot bath and food, and decided that warnings about strangers could hardly apply to a gentleman like Sir Colin, who was already an old and trusted friend, anyway. Besides, what was the alternative? "Well, all right," she agreed. "But, you know, it isn't at all proper. You won't tell anyone, will you?"

Sir Colin laughed suddenly, a delicious, deeply amused chuckle. "No, I promise not to tell a soul," he said, and lifted her from the horse.

It was a fine rich house, with new bright tapestries on all the walls, and a new carved table. But it wasn't until Kitty the maid had helped her to freshen up and she had satisfied her hunger that Linnet looked at it with much attention. It was much more elaborately adorned than Fontenay, and rather too grand for Linnet's taste. But then, this was London.

She yawned. Sir Colin had served her a goblet of very sweet wine, with no water added, quite as if she were grown up. But it was making her sleepy, and she was already tired from a day of walking and riding. She stretched her eyelids widely.

"I've decided what we'd best do," she announced. "You can just take me to see Queen Bess, and she'll find my cousins for me. She and Mother were best friends when they were thirteen, and—"

"You're jesting!" he interrupted with a laugh that suggested he was finding her just a trifle less amusing than he had. "My dear young minx, do you know what you're asking? Do you know how complicated it is to get an audience with the Queen? Do you even know where she is?"

Linnet blinked. "Well, at Whitehall Palace, isn't she?"

"Possibly. Or perhaps at another palace. Hampton Court, or Nonesuch, or Windsor, or Greenwich, or Eltham, or possibly on one of her Progressions: say in Dorset or Kent or Gloucestershire." He cocked his pointed beard at her and grinned. "I'm no magician, my dear. Besides, I have a much better idea. Sit down and listen to it."

Linnet sat politely on the stool he indicated, but her wayward eyebrow leveled itself in a manner suggesting that she was going to be obstinate. She had no mind to do anything at all but what she chose.

"How would you like to stay and visit me until we find your cousins?" he asked her with a smile that was both charming and reasonable.

"Well, I don't think I'd better," said Linnet at once. "I've already told you, it—"

"Yes, yes; I remember," he interrupted hastily. "Not proper. But you'll be quite safe, you know; and considering that I gave you my nuncheon, don't you think you should do something to please me?"

"As soon as I find my cousins, we'll invite you to dinner," she told him kindly. "And Mother and Father will want to meet you, too, as soon as they know all about it."

"Aye, I'm sure of that," he agreed with such dry amusement that Linnet stared. A guffaw from the footman was cut short by a sharp glance from his master, and Linnet stared harder. What very odd servants! She began to feel just slightly uneasy.

"If you don't mind, I think I'll go right away," she announced, standing up.

"But I do mind," said her host smoothly. He gestured, and a pair of hands pressed firmly upon her shoulders and sat her down again.

She leaned forward and twisted her head, to see the footman who had laughed standing behind her stool, looking amused. Neither his face nor his manner was at all fitting to his station in life, which, as everyone knew, was about halfway between horses and gentry; not quite animal, but definitely of the lower orders of humanity.

"How dare you?" she fumed. "Sir Colin, don't your servants know their places?"

"They obey my orders," he replied evenly. "Now turn around, young minx, and listen to me. I'm going to put my invitation in different words. You are my guest as long as I choose to keep you so. Is that perfectly clear?"

Linnet started to bounce up with a squeal of rage and alarm. The hands pushed her down once more. She instantly slithered all the way to the floor in a tangle of kirtle and petticoat, rolled over once, scrambled to her feet just out of reach of the surprised footman, and with a rip of stood-on lace, her full skirts bunched in her hands, rushed toward the door. Another servant appeared in it, blocking her way, and Kitty behind him. There was no chance at all of getting past. Moreover, Linnet was feeling extraordinarily odd. Noises swelled and boomed in an unreal way, and everything looked peculiarly dreamlike. Bewildered, she half turned back toward Sir Colin.

"You're teasing me, aren't you?" she suggested doubtfully. And then she felt hideously dizzy, and the floor swooped toward her in an outrageous manner. And then she stopped noticing anything at all, because someone hit her on the head.

She awoke painfully and coldly and in utter bewilderment. Why did her head hurt, and what was this dank, evil-smelling place? She squinted into the dimness, lit only by a small, high unglassed window. It was a barren garret of a room, containing only a single three-legged stool, and a slop-jar, and the unsavory pallet on which she lay. Ridiculous! She closed her eyes again, certain she was ill of a fever.

"Nell!" she croaked peevishly. "Mother! Cecy!" And then the sound of her own voice caused her to remember everything—and to wish passionately that she didn't. Oblivion was much to be preferred, particularly when one's head ached so badly.

Her call was answered by a creaking door and a hoarse girl-voice in the strange London accents she had heard on the streets last night. (Was it last night?) " 'Oo yer calling, luv? Me name's not Nell, 'tis Nan."

Linnet focused painfully between waves of nausea, and finally made out a gaunt, ragged figure. It knelt beside her pallet, and an equally gaunt and grimy face appeared half hidden amid wildly uncombed dirty brown hair. A foolish smile displayed blackened teeth with a gaping space here and there, and Linnet drew away in revulsion.

"Don't be afeared," said Nan earnestly. "I won't 'urt yer. Nobody won't 'urt yer if Colley says not, 'owever much they wants. They dassn't. 'E'd slit their gizzards."

"Huh?" asked Linnet, blank.

"We all does wot Colley says," Nan explained. " 'E's the Upright Man. See?"

Linnet didn't. She'd never heard of such a thing, and grunted questioningly and querulously.

" 'E's the cleverest and strongest and 'ardest, so 'e's the Upright Man and we all does wotever 'e says," Nan repeated carefully. "If 'e said ter kill yer, us would. But 'e said ter take care of yer," she added reassuringly. " 'N if 'e said ter take care of yer, 'e don't want yer 'urt, does 'e?" She patted Linnet's head and looked terribly pleased with herself for figuring out this complicated bit of reasoning.

Linnet winced, partly from being patted on her headache, but also partly at being touched by this dirty idiot of a girl who was far too stupid to know that she was distasteful.

"Yer 'ead 'urts!" Nan discovered sympathetically, seeing the wince. "Coo, there's a big lump on it! That must be where Gregory 'it yer," she concluded with the pride of one who just made her second brilliant deduction in as many minutes. " 'E's turble strong, Gregory be. It'll go down soon. Be yer 'ungry?"

"No!" said Linnet as forcefully as she could without causing her head to break instantly into separate pieces. As it was, she could feel it crack threateningly. "I'm cold," she whimpered rather less forcefully. "And I'm thirsty. And I demand to be taken home. Or to Giles. Or to the Queen . . . Or somewhere. . . ." she finished in tones about as commanding as those of a baby rabbit.

"Well, I can't do that," Nan told her comfortably. "But I'll get yer somefing ter drink and 'appen a bit of blanket, and a wet rag for yer 'ead, and then you'll feel better, see if yer don't."

In no condition to argue, Linnet closed her eyes, and presently submitted to a cold cloth on the head, a grimy blanket, and a single spoonful of a hot but revolting broth.

"I thought yer might like somefing ter eat," said Nan benevolently, spooning it into Linnet's feebly resisting mouth.

"Ugh!" sputtered Linnet, turning her head away at infinite risk of it falling off. "No more!"

"Not 'ungry?" Nan began to gulp the rejected offering. " 'Twas me own supper," she confessed. "But I thought yer ought ter 'ave it if yer wanted it." She went away contentedly.

When she returned an hour later, Linnet was shivering violently, from cold, shock, fear, and the blow on the head. Nan stared at her in concern. It seemed clear that the little lady was far from well. But Colley had said she was to be kept prisoner in that room until he returned. And Colley's commands were never questioned. Nan considered. She didn't think Colley would like the prisoner to die, but he had neglected to give any commands about what to do should she seem ill. No use asking anyone else. Joan wouldn't care, and Maudlin wouldn't say, and the others wouldn't know, even if they were here. And most of them were either at work or in gaol. Clearly things were up to Nan.

Linnet's teeth were chattering. Nan held the rushlight closer and by the feeble flicker of its light she could see that the greenish eyes were glazed and nearly closed; the freckled face very white; and the lips bluish. It seemed to Nan that the best thing to do would be to get the young lady warm. Encouraged by this idea, she went and fetched all of her own clothing and every ragged blanket or cloak she could find, piled them on top of Linnet, crawled in beside her, hugged the shivering figure close, and having done all she could think of, slept.

"She hasn't gone home!" insisted Giles. "I tell you, she's run away!"

His parents looked at him helplessly. Giles was such a strong-minded lad! As strong-minded if not quite as wayward as their god-daughter Linnet. In a way, things were rather easier when the two of them were together and could take out all that energy on each other, and it was going to be a great relief when they were old enough to marry, which was clearly inevitable. After all, who else could possibly stand up to either of them?

"But Giles," said his father patiently, "she said she was going home. Her note says—" He began to read. " 'I have decyded to gowe homme alonge with Sir Guy after alle, and ther bee no tyme to saye farewelle or pakke, for he be leavynge presently so I bid thee goode den and faire ye welle, and I shalle send anon for myne clothynge.' "

Giles snorted. "You don't really believe that, do you?"

"Of course," said Sir Henry, mystified. "Why not? Where else would she have gone?"

"To London," returned his son.

His father shook his head, but his mother frowned thoughtfully. She knew Linnet better than Sir Henry did. "It was odd, of course, to change her mind so suddenly, and not even stop to say farewell, but if she decided just as he was riding off, 'twould be just like her. And surely, my dear son—"

"London!" repeated her dear son grimly. "She's been talking of little else this last month; you know that. Ever since she heard that Edward Seymour is to be wed this summer. She wants to be an attendant—"

"To Beauchamp?" His father looked startled. "But surely she knows there's no love lost between that branch of Seymours and her father's?"

"She won't believe it's serious," said Giles. "Thinks everything will be reconciled the minute she appears. You know how she is! Moreover, she'd never have left her things here if she'd been going home; she'd have kept Sir Guy waiting half a day whilst she packed them. The only reason she'd leave them here is if she's running away to London, and counting on her noble cousins to furnish her with more and finer clothes, and jewels."

They stared, aghast. "She wouldn't! Giles, not even Linnet would do anything so mad!"

"She would. You know she would. She has, I tell you!" Giles stood with his feet planted apart, looking, as usual, as ordinary a boy as one could imagine. He was comfortably average in height, with nice blue eyes and hair that had once been fair but was now getting darker, and a straight nose, and ears that just slightly stuck out, giving him a mildly inquisitive air. His parents looked at him anxiously.

"I don't like the look in your eye, Giles," said his mother uneasily. "What have you decided to do, and don't you think you should have consulted your father and me before deciding it?"

"I'm going to London to find her."

They looked at him, appalled. "You don't even know she's there!"

"I know she started for there," he told them stubbornly. "I hope to catch up before she gets very far. She's such a gullible chit, there's just no telling what trouble she might get into. Probably has already," he added gloomily. "Now don't worry about me, Mother; I know London well enough, and I shall take Wat and Ned along, and go stay with Lord Crowden. Last time they were here, he invited me to come visit him and Hugh whenever I please. Remember?"

Sir Henry shifted his gouty foot and took a firm grip on reality. "My dear Giles, I sometimes think you're as fanciful as Linnet, and rather more headstrong. She's safely on her way home, you may be sure of it. No, no; prithee don't argue. Go ahead, since you're so set on it, and have a good time in London. You and young Hugh have always got along well, and he might have a calming effect on you. But you mustn't expect us to start writing frantic letters to Tom and Robin, for their daughter will reach them long before any letters could, and they'll only think we've quite lost our reason."

Giles frowned. Then he thought again and shrugged. Perhaps, after all, it was best not to alarm Linnet's family yet. Perhaps he'd find her still on the road. In any case, there was little they could do that he and Hugh—and Hugh's father, of course—couldn't do sooner. Yes, better to wait.

"All right," he agreed suddenly, rather to their surprise. "Don't fret yourselves, then, but I'm off at once. Tell cook to put up some food for us, will you, Mother? In half an hour, please." And he left the room so abruptly that he seemed to leave a vacuum behind.

3

The Upright Man

When Linnet was again able to think at all, she found herself torn between disbelief and fury. Mostly disbelief. The dingy room was so altogether unlikely that if she shut her eyes she could easily think it was all imagi— She jumped, scratched violently, and flung herself off the filthy pallet, still scratching. It wasn't a nightmare at all! It was as real as louse-bites could make it! Real as the shabby, dirty chemise and petticoats that had replaced the fine clothes she had been wearing. Real as the sounds of footsteps up rickety stairs. . . .

Linnet snatched at the grimy gray blanket on the pallet, wrapped it around herself, and glared at the door, which was making sounds of being unbolted. Her head had stopped aching and she was filled with a great wrath and a number of things she wanted to say to Sir Colin.

And Sir Colin obligingly appeared, wearing an aura of good humor about him—and also wearing, confusingly, the sober trunk-hose and furred gown of a respectable London merchant instead of the gentleman's dress he had worn before. Linnet regarded him with hatred.

"How dare you?" she exploded. "Give me my things back and let me go at once, you wicked knave! You're a liar and a scoundrel and a rogue, and what's more," she decided vehemently, "I don't believe you're really a gentleman at all!"

Sir Colin looked startled. Then he threw back his head and laughed. "Why, 'tis a spirited bird I've netted!" he observed approvingly. "More like a cheeky sparrow than a linnet! Well, well, so much the better!"

Linnet stared at him. If it wasn't a dream, then it had to be a mistake or a joke—or perhaps there was some perfectly sensible explanation. There had to be! She valiantly swallowed the lump in her throat and reminded herself that she frequently imagined dire things, and they usually turned out not dire at all, or if they were, she and Giles were in them together and could help each other out of trouble. But this really was by far the direst thing she had ever imagined, and Giles wasn't with her at all, but in Guildford and thinking her safely on the way home.

It was a joke! It must be. That was why Sir Colin was laughing.

"I don't think it's the least bit funny," she told him coldly.

Sir Colin said nothing. He merely seated himself on the tottery three-legged stool, leaned against the patched gray wall, and laughed and laughed, while Linnet regarded him with increasing anger.

"I do wish you'd stop that!" she snapped. " 'Tis very bad manners to go on laughing when the other person can't see the joke, and I'm the other person, and I don't see it at all, and nor would you if you were me. You're behaving like a vile knave!"

He wiped his eyes, nearly went off into another peal,

and controlled himself. "I do beg your pardon, Sparrow," he said politely. "As a matter of fact, I am a vile knave. I told you so when we met, if you'll remember, and you wouldn't believe me. 'Tis very discouraging, you know. I hardly ever tell the truth, and when I do, 'tis disbelieved. You've disillusioned me so that I may never try it again."

"Oh, I'm sorry," Linnet began, and then stopped. His eyes were twinkling in the most disconcerting way, and she was no longer quite so sure that it was a nice twinkle.

"Don't go on teasing me in that horrid way!" she begged. "I know it's a joke—but—" She stopped. He was regarding her with the quizzical smile she was beginning to detest, and shaking his head slightly. Panic leaped again into Linnet's throat, and she stared wide-eyed.

"But—but, why? I've never done anything to you except eat your goose, and you gave me that; and you mustn't go around hitting people on the head and stealing them away and locking them up in horrid dirty places with bugs! And besides," she remembered with a fresh sense of grievance, "that stupid Nan-girl said you were an upright man, and she's quite wrong, for anyone less upright and honest than you I never saw in my life. You deceived me!"

This had the effect of sending him off into laughter again. Linnet sat very still and straight, clutching the dirty blanket around her and staring at him with the sense of nightmare so strong that she was able to wonder at her own calm.

He stopped laughing and sat regarding her thoughtfully for a moment. When he spoke again, it was in the grave and courteous tones of yesterday.

"Lackaday, I do beg your pardon for my ill manners, Sparrow," he said. "You'll forgive me, won't you?"

"I will if you'll bring back my clothes and take me to my cousins," she said promptly, cheering up.

He shook his head again, regretful but firm, over folded arms. "Now why should I go to all the trouble of stealing you just to take you back again, Sparrow?" he asked.

"I'm not Sparrow, I'm Linnet. I think you might at least remember my name! And I do wish you'd stop sounding like my family being reasonable, because that's what you're not being. Even the wickedest people ought to have a reason for doing vile things, besides just being vile and wicked, you know."

She blinked back sudden tears.

"But I have got a reason," he told her. "Now don't start crying, Sparrow," he went on hastily, seeing that her lip was starting to quiver. "You know, 'tis most monstrous churlish of you not even to listen to my explanation." He looked hurt and reproachful, thereby at once putting Linnet in the wrong again.

"Well, I'm sorry, but I can't help it" she sniffled. "And besides, you haven't explained anything except that you did it on purpose and you won't take me back, and I still don't see why anyone should call you an upright man."

"Please don't start me laughing again!" he begged, still imperviously good-natured. How Linnet wished she could pierce that armor and banish the smile! Clearly, futile anger wouldn't. And now, disarmingly, he was talking as if she were a grown lady and his trusted friend. Despite herself, Linnet listened.

"I will be quite candid with you, my dear," he said.

"When Nan calls me the Upright Man, she means that I'm King of the underworld."

Linnet frowned, puzzled. "Underworld? You mean like Hades when he stole poor Persephone? But that's only an old Greek myth, you know, and you needn't think—"

He clutched at his hair in a way that people frequently did when they had been talking to Linnet for a while. "Stubble it, Sparrow!" he groaned. "Hold your tongue, do, and let me explain. The underworld, my dear, is the part of London that your class wouldn't know about. The poor and criminal. The people who beg or steal; those who don't know any other trade, and those who don't want to. The Upright Man is their king, who trains and protects them when he can, and arranges begging licenses— genuine or forged. He's the head of the thieves' guild, if you choose. Does that shock you?"

"Well, it most certainly does!" Linnet's eyes were round and horrified. "Why, that's not honest! And don't you dare laugh at me again," she warned him, for his lip was twitching once more. " 'Tis perfectly true and not a bit funny!"

"No, it's not funny," he agreed, suddenly serious again. "Tell me, Sparrow, what do you think all those people who must either steal or starve should do? Starve?"

She blinked and refused to be sidetracked. "Well, I don't know, but I'm perfectly sure 'tis wrong to steal. And I still don't see what it's got to do with me, because I'm not a beggar or thief or of the lower orders at all. What do you want with me?"

He surveyed her for a long moment, his eyes narrowed and thoughtful. Linnet stared back sullenly. Whatever he wanted, she decided, she would have nothing to do with it.

"It was your own idea, really," he told her suddenly.

"It wasn't!" She stiffened in renewed indignation. "I never—"

"Didn't you say you wanted to help save Queen Bess from the Papist plotters?" he demanded, accusing. "Or were you just saying it because it sounded well?"

"No! Yes! I mean, well of course I do, but—"

"Well, that's precisely what I mean to let you do!" He beamed at her as one bestowing a rare favor, and confident that she could never refuse it. Nor could she.

"Truly?" she demanded. "Well, why didn't you say so? Tell me about it at once! Is it France or Spain or the Pope or Queen Mary or all of them? The idea, pretending Mary has a right to the throne when she's only the grand-daughter of Queen Bess's aunt! Father says Mary always claims she doesn't know a thing about any of the plots, but—"

"Do you want to hear about this one or not?" he demanded. Linnet blinked and nodded. "Then close your chaffer," he commanded cheerfully. Linnet blinked again in the dimness, but by now everything was so unlikely that it all seemed almost ordinary, so she sighed and hugged the blanket about her and subsided.

"As a matter of fact, I can't tell you much about it at all," he confessed shamelessly, and then raised a graceful hand as Linnet began to bristle. "Now don't get in a tweak, Sparrow; if I knew all about it, I wouldn't need you. It's simply that in my—er—role as a gentleman named Sir Colin, I've become quite friendly with some of our leading Roman Catholic families, especially the Throckmortons."

Linnet curled her lip. "Don't sneer, Sparrow, they have the virtue of loyal steadfastness—to their religion if not to their Queen and country. One must choose, I suppose. Walsingham, of course, would like to have all their ilk executed at once, but—"

"So should I!" agreed Linnet at once.

"But Queen Elizabeth won't hear of it," he finished blandly, shaking his head at such regrettable soft-heartedness. "So, as I say, I'm friends with them, but not trusted enough to be confided in, or even to visit as frequently as I'd like. Now, 'tis just possible you could be of some help there. . . ." He trailed off into a reflective silence, while Linnet sat enthralled and expectant, her coppery hair a rippled mantle over the foulness of the blanket. There was an odd expression in Sir Colin's eyes as he looked at her, but Linnet didn't notice this, for she was thrilling to being at last treated as a responsible grown-up and told important things. She warmed to him again. However badly he had behaved, at least it was from the best of possible reasons.

"What am I to do?" she asked, as the silence continued.

He came out of his thoughts. "Do? Well, now, wait a bit. There are preparations to make. You'll bide here for a while like a good girl, won't you?"

But Linnet's restored approval and tractability didn't extend to accepting lice and bedbugs cheerfully. Her face darkened. "Well, I don't see why," she objected rebelliously. "And I don't see why you had to steal me and hit me on the head and put me here, either, when you might have just simply asked me to help, you know. No gentleman should ever behave in such a cullionly way!"

"As a matter of fact, I'm not a gentleman," he admitted with his charming smile. "The Sir Colin is a fiction, as well as Collyngewood Hall. My friends call me Colley."

Linnet digested this. "Oh. Well, but you still haven't explained why you brought me to this vile place. I don't at all wish to stay here. Why can't I stay at Over House?"

He stood up with sudden briskness. "I'm sorry, Sparrow, but there are reasons why I can't keep you in Over House. Don't pout, my dear; it doesn't become you. You must believe that I know what I'm doing. Don't you trust me?"

"Well, yes," she said reluctantly, "though I can't think why I do. But I don't want to stay here! I hate it, and it's not the sort of place for a lady."

Colley sighed and wondered whatever had given him the notion that docility would follow trust. He had noticed the other night that the two didn't necessarily go together, and that although this child was so trusting as to be foolish, she was also exceedingly stubborn.

"I shan't argue the point," he said in a voice used to commanding. "You'll stay here, Sparrow, and get acquainted with my Flock. I think it will broaden your outlook, you know."

"I don't want it broadened." Linnet hugged the offensive blanket closer about her, feeling suddenly cold despite the tiny slit of summer sky showing in the window gap above a rooftop. "And I don't know what you mean by Flock."

"They're my scholars and apprentices," he told her jovially. "Didn't I tell you I had a school for knavery?"

"I'm not going to live with people like that!" she bleated, standing up abruptly. "I'll go home, and not help you at all!"

"You'd refuse to help save your Queen?" He looked shocked. Linnet sat down again, deflated and feeling that somehow she was being maneuvered in a way she couldn't quite put her finger on. "Besides," he added with great gentleness, "you can't go home without my help. You're in the midst of the London underworld, Sparrow. If you leave without escort, you'd be quite likely to find yourself a corpse in the Thames, that might or might not be washed ashore somewhere down-river."

Linnet simply stared at him, horror in her eyes. He nodded affably. "Aye. So be a good little Sparrow and do as I say."

"No!" said Linnet at once.

He arose. "Oh, I think you'll change your mind, my dear. I must off about my business now, and you just make yourself at home. Nan's finding you some clothing; you'll wear that for the nonce and keep your pretty things for later."

"No," said Linnet again, rather less decisively.

"Oh, yes, you will. And perhaps you can amuse yourself by teaching upper-class manners to my Flock; it might be very useful to them. Just put your mind to it, and you'll quite enjoy your stay here, Sparrow."

"No," wailed Linnet, and burst into tears.

4

Giles

"I rode hard for London to try to overtake her," said Giles. "I kept Wat with me, and left Ned to follow more slowly, asking along the way. But I haven't found a trace, and—"

"Soft you, now," said Lord Crowden soothingly. "You'll put your wits awry if you go on like that." He waved at Giles's flushed face. "You have too much choler, belike; it goes to the head. Were you born under a Fire sign? Aries, perhaps, or Leo, or even Sagittarius? You should be bled now and then, lad; a little blood-letting would calm you down most wondrously. Still, as you're so upset about this girl. . . . Do you really want me to send a messenger to her parents?"

Giles's nod was unnecessary; his face said it for him. It wore a look of implacable obstinacy that always caused those who knew him well to sigh and give way.

Lord Crowden did likewise. "Oh, very well. Though we'll find, I warrant, that she's safe at home by now, and all your excitement for nought. To tell you the truth, I don't see what makes you think she ran away at all; you haven't a shred of real evidence, you know."

Giles turned his head to stare out of the window. Lord

Crowden's was one of the splendid great houses just west of London Town, on the Strand. The gardens and southern windows overlooked the Thames with its bustle of traffic, but this northern room looked over the busy road between London and Whitehall Palace, and to the row of mean houses across the road. He didn't really see them. He was wondering how to explain how he knew about Linnet without any need for evidence. What he had instead was his intuition about her.

He had always had this, since the summer he was seven and had gone to visit his godparents, and first met the four-year-old Linnet who was already showing signs of driving her family straight into Bedlam. It wasn't that she was naughty, really. Giles had understood this at once, even though he couldn't have put it into words. It was merely that she had a nature that was at once adventurous, literal-minded, and trusting. As a consequence, she believed everything anyone said or did, and never looked before she leaped. And if people told her contradictory things, she simply kept them in separate compartments in her mind, and never compared them, and went by whichever one most suited her mood at the moment.

Moreover, as Colley was in the process of discovering, she was not a tractable girl; and anyone silly enough to suppose females were naturally lacking in spirit or inventiveness or brains, clearly did not know either Queen Bess or Linnet. . . . Though it was true that Linnet had not as yet altogether learned to curb her headstrong impulses with a little common sense. She was always getting into scrapes, which considerably brightened Giles's life— though he would not have told her so for worlds.

By now, with ten years' practice, he knew her mind almost as if he lived in it, and he knew she had run off to London—or at least started out with that intention. But how could he explain this to Lord Crowden and Hugh, who simply didn't have that sort of imagination?

He sighed. "I'll be most grateful, Sir, if you will send the message," he said.

"Of course, of course," said Lord Crowden, instantly turning his attention to other matters. "I'll tell Crumley. Now forget this nonsense, and you boys enjoy yourselves. Go hawking. Go riding. Go courting. See if Amy Throckmorton's back in town yet." He winked at his son, who grinned a trifle sheepishly.

"She isn't," said Hugh.

"Ah well, there are other girls. Belike you know most of them." He left the room with a jovial nod, hoping Hugh could take young Giles's mind off this silly notion of his.

Giles flicked his blue eyes at Hugh, and turned to stare out of the window again. The Strand was busier and more built-up than last time he was here. London was almost visibly spreading beyond its walls, like moss over paving stones or a pool steadily overflowing its banks, further and further in all directions. Some day, doubtless, it would creep all the way westward along Fleet Street and down the Strand, and might even engulf the village of Charing Cross, or Whitehall itself. Already it was overcrowded. And in all those throngs of people—Giles set his lips and pushed a wave of sick fear back down again. If only his intuition could be more precise!

Hugh had been sitting on a three-legged stool, chin propped in palms, staring at his mother's cherished new bulb-legged table as if wondering what the world was coming to now that boards on trestles were no longer good enough. As a matter of fact, he hadn't been noticing the table at all. He had been thinking. Having thought, he now raised a brooding eye to his friend.

"A pox on it," he pronounced. "You're a jobbernowl, Giles; the girl can't have come here at all. It wouldn't be sensible. She'd have to be mad even to consider it."

"She is," Giles told him simply. "Hugh, do you know all the Seymour family?"

Hugh stared. He was a short, stocky boy, with a bulldog chin and an altogether misleading look of unyielding doggedness. He had a strong aversion to anything at all disagreeable or even requiring much effort.

"No more than I can help," he answered. "Don't like 'em. Why?"

"Linnet's related to them, dolt. I'm sure that's where she'd go, if she reached London. The Earl of Hertford is out in the provinces somewhere still trying to get back in grace with Her Majesty, and his sons said they hadn't heard anything of Linnet and didn't seem to know she existed at all. But what about Hertford's mother and sisters and brother? Come on, get your cloak; you're going to take me to visit as many as we can find."

Hugh looked unhappy. "Don't like 'em, I tell you. Don't even know some of 'em, and don't want to. Anyhow, you don't want to go visiting at this hour. I thought we were going hawking."

Giles upset the stool and dumped him off, with no regard whatever for the fine new trunk-hose of apple green slashed with lilac and saffron. "Come on!" he said.

5

Nether 'Ouse

"That's better," said Colley, smiling kindly at Linnet in the shabby and none-too-clean attire Nan had provided. " 'Tis almost a smile."

" 'Tisn't!" said Linnet at once. "I'm tried of being locked up in this filthy room! When do I start foiling the plot against the Queen? That's really the only reason I'm—"

"Leave it all to me," said Colley, so confidently and with such a benevolent smile that she was almost mollified. Not that it would do to let him know it, of course. He was much too masterful. In fact, now she came to think of it, he was much bossier than Giles and not nearly so nice. It was true that he was rather more tactful on the whole, but— Linnet found that she very much wished Giles were with her. However horrid he was at times, she had got used to having him around, and adventures were not quite the same without him to share them and make insulting remarks.

"Now I shall show you the house and my Flock," said Colley, still kindly and masterful. "You'll see what a gentle shepherd I am."

"I think you're a villainous carbuncle and a pernicious

caitiff," Linnet informed him briskly, borrowing some of her mother's truly impressive vocabulary.

Colley looked hurt. "How ungrateful of you, when I'm giving you hospitality, and devoting my precious time to showing you around, and I've even promised to let you help save the Queen from her enemies. Really, Sparrow, you wound me deeply."

"Well, I'm sorry," began Linnet uncertainly, a little dashed by this. Was she behaving in a thankless manner? "But you did put me here to start with, and lock me up, when I don't want to live in this house at all," she reminded him defensively.

He chuckled, and opened the door for her with a flourish and bow suitable for a Duchess. "You haven't seen it yet," he reminded her reasonably. "Only one room. Now here is the girls' wardrobe room." He indicated a large dim chamber filled with chests and boxes, and with assorted clothing hanging from walls and beams in an astonishing manner. "Beyond is another for males. We have all kinds of outfit here, to produce anyone from beggar to merchant, shopkeeper to noble lord or lady."

Linnet regarded the room dubiously. It was dark and cobwebby, and it was doubtful if it had been swept for years. Moreover, she strongly suspected that the costumes were not used for honest purposes. In fact, she was almost certain of it, for Colley had all but told her as much.

"Just because someone's lower class," she said primly, "he needn't be dishonest, you know."

Colley gave her an odd look, but did not answer. Instead he led the way out to the landing of a rickety tangle of stairs and pointed upwards. "Next floor up is the boys' dormitory, and the top floor is the girls," he said. "You'll join my kynchin morts there from now on, Sparrow, and find it much more companionable than that little closet, I feel sure."

Linnet was regarding the walls suspiciously. They were made of good stout half-timbered wattle-and-daub, but they must have had at least one or two hundred years of hard wear, with no plaster or paint for the last fifty, and they tended to sag and bulge here and there in a manner she didn't at all like. So did the floors, for that matter, while the stairs were worn deep with many feet. She tore her apprehensive stare from this to answer Colley with deep feeling.

"Well, I don't know what kynchin morts may be, but if they live here, I feel quite sure I won't like their company at all; and mind you, I won't be one, either, whatever you say."

"Certainly not," he agreed, leading the way down the twisting stairs. "You're my gentry mort."

It didn't sound much better. Linnet scowled, but then her attention was diverted, for they had reached the bottom of the stairs and were in a narrow corridor that was like a maze. It opened on one side, twisted to another, and erupted suddenly into an entry hall with another corridor to the right, and a door to the left.

"Cock's bones!" she said, using Giles's favorite expression. " 'Tis like a puzzle box, or the maze Mother told me of at Hampton Court."

"Exactly!" Colley seemed pleased. "To confuse any unwanted visitors. Come, I'll show you." He led the way down the other corridor, which turned once and ran along the front wall to the outer door. Colley stood Linnet with her back to the door. "Now, you've just come in from the light, and have never seen it before," he said. "Which way would you go?"

The corridor they had just come down was a small opening over on her right, almost behind the door when it was open. Directly ahead was a much wider one. Linnet jerked her head at it without hesitation.

"Aye, marry!" Colley laughed. "Come and see where it leads."

Where it led was confusing. Sharply to the left, sharply to the right, and then apparently into a blank wall with some old planks leaning against it, and a bottomless bucket, some rags, and other bits of assorted junk. But it wasn't a dead end, after all. At the last possible moment, the corridor did an abrupt turn-about on itself, went back the way it came, made several zig-zags, and emerged at the bottom of the stairs they had come down a few minutes earlier.

Linnet blinked. "Well, if the whole idea is to confuse your guests, I should think it would do it splendidly," she observed. "But I must say it doesn't seem very hospitable."

"It isn't," he said, greatly pleased at her reaction, and went back into the entry hall and from there through a door into the main downstairs room. "Our Great Hall," he smiled, waving his hand gracefully. "Common room, schoolroom, kitchen and dining room, solar, and parlor."

The floor was deep with rushes, which had apparently been brought in now and then over the past century or so, but had never been removed. Linnet had frequently thought her mother quite unnecessarily fussy about changing the rushes every fortnight; now she suddenly saw her point very strongly indeed. She tried not to imagine what might be at the bottom layer; it was bad enough to smell it.

"What a vile stinking place!" she commented with her usual candor. "You can't possibly really mean for me to stay here; why, 'tisn't fit even for beggars!"

Colley looked at her, surprised. "You haven't the least notion what you're talking about, Sparrow. This place is sheer luxury for my Flock. Wait until you've seen the kennels and gutters and alleys most of them came from."

"Well, I don't want to see them!" Linnet's pointed chin was looking obstinate. "I don't even want to think about them. You'll just have to find a suitable place for me, that's all."

Colley raised an eyebrow at her. It wasn't a particularly sympathetic eyebrow, however good-natured. "I tell you, Sparrow, you must stay here, and do as I say. Now just sit down and take another good look around, my dear."

"No," said Linnet automatically, but did. There wasn't much to see. A narrow window on the front wall let in what light there was. Along the middle of the long side wall was a fireplace, with a meager fire tended by a gaunt, gray-haired, middle-aged woman who hadn't even glanced up. Now and then she stirred at a large simmering pot, filled with pease porridge and perhaps some half-rotten scraps of meat by the smell of it.

"That's Maudlin," Colley said. "She's housemother. She hardly ever says a word, but she keeps an eye on the kynchin morts, tends the sores, cooks, helps train the little ones, prevents Peace and Salamon from killing each other, and puts a hand to the housekeeping."

Linnet stared around with a critical greenish eye. "She doesn't put *much* of a hand to the housekeeping," she observed. "Nobody does. 'Tis a disgrace."

This earned her a brief unfriendly glance from Maudlin and a waggled finger from Colley. "How, now, Sparrow, keep your chaffer closed or you'll end up in a prime tweak one of these days."

She stared. "Is that thieves' cant you're talking? Giles told me rogues in London had a special language of their own, but I can't speak it; how could I? How am I supposed to know what you're saying?"

"You'll pick it up," he told her, grinning. "Even though you're only a gentry mort. In return, you can teach some of my kynchin morts fine gentry manners, mayhap."

"No!" snapped Linnet, outraged.

The infuriating Colley actually seemed amused by this, remarking jovially that he did like spirit in a female—within limits, of course—and if she shaped up well, he might even make her his doxy one of these days.

Linnet didn't quite know what a doxy might be, but she didn't at all like the sound of it. She subsided into gloomy and sullen silence on her narrow bench, while the squalor and chill of the house and the despair of having to stay there even a short time sank into her bones. She hardly noticed at first when the outer door began groaning open and banging shut, and people began arriving in the common room from the maze of corridors. Then her eyes began to focus again and she stared.

They were a motley lot, mostly young. Children of four or five stopped limping as they came into the room, and began fishing coppers from assorted hiding places among their rags. These they put on the table, either sheepishly or proudly according to the amount. Several whipped foul rags off ugly open sores and examined the latter with a professional air.

"Need more lye on this," announced a small urchin in disgust, showing it to Colley. "Nubbody wasn't upset when I showed it. Salamon's is lots better, innit?"

A few older ones were neatly and respectably dressed, and these produced—or failed to produce—neatly cut purses. A flock of grown girls blew in giggling and proceeded to show Colley how Joan had batted her eyes at a swell cove until he was fair befuddled whilst Polly picked his pocket neat as cods.

"Colley, Colley, Colley!" clamored a moppet with a tangle of curls the color of straw that had been all winter on a stable floor. "Listen! Look!" Her voice had simply incredible volume, and she had the personality of a major battle. "I got me 'and in the pocket wivout ringing the bells three times last night, so that makes me a foister, dunnit?"

Colley laughed. "One thing to get your hand in, Peace my poppet, and quite another to get anything out. Let's see you try it now."

The child went over to the darkest corner, where Linnet noticed for the first time there were a number of purses and pockets hanging from hooks. They seemed to have dozens of tiny hawkbells sewed all over them. Moving with most impressive care, Peace got her hand quite into one of them and was fishing for something when one of the bells tinkled. She swore luridly, and the others laughed.

"Yaaah!" jeered Salamon, a sandy-haired urchin with buck teeth and a snub nose. "Can't even pick a pocket!

Wants to be a foister afore she's 'ardly a nipper, silly dell!"

Peace at once made a strenuous effort to kill him. They rolled over the floor, biting and kicking, clawing and screaming. Linnet, recoiling from the ferocity of it, gathered that this must be a regular event, for the others paid little attention. But at length the battle rolled against a long-legged young man called Diggory, who picked them up, each by the scruff of a dirty neck, shook them, bumped their heads together until they yowled, and set them down again. Salamon wandered over to sniff at the simmering pot, forgetting all about the fight, and Peace instantly prepared to attack Diggory.

"Come here, Peace," ordered Colley, apparently feeling that enough was enough. "Try that pocket again. The rest of you, too."

"Me next! No, me!" A clamor of children, shoving and pinching, lined up for the nightly practice. It was clear that they loved the game. Eyes sparkled and laughter bubbled. Colley directed, rewarding each with a jest, a cuff, a word of praise or encouragement.

Linnet, watching with astonished eyes, sat forgotten in her dim corner until a warm stench snuggled itself next to her with shy boldness. Nan was suffering a fierce attack of hero-worship. That Linnet was a great lady she had seen instantly and with awe. She had never been addressed by such a being before, much less had the honor of feeding and tending one, and soothing its headache. Now she sidled slightly closer and peered sideways at Linnet, perfectly certain of a snub, but minding no more than a devoted puppy would.

44

Linnet edged away, wrinkling her nose. Although it was an accepted fact of nature that people tended to stink, surely there were limits?

"Don't you ever wash?" she demanded, looking at the grayish skin of Nan's thin face.

Nan looked shocked. "Make yer sick," she explained kindly. "Not natural, warshing. Like takin' off nits 'n lice. Nits 'n lice 'n dirt's 'ealthy," she added. "You'll be 'ealthier when yer gets more."

"I done it, Colley! D'yer see? I done it! I'm a proper prig, I am! I'm a foister! Can I try it tomorrow on a flash cove, Colley?"

"What is she talking about?" Linnet demanded of Nan. "What's a nipper and a foister and a flash cove and a kynchin mort? And a gentry mort?" she added, remembering a certain remark of Colley's.

Nan looked astounded at such ignorance. "A gentry mort's a lady, like yer," she explained. " 'N a nipper's a cutpurse, 'n a foister's a pickpocket; that's 'arder, yer see. 'N when someone gets better nor a prig—that's a robber —they moves to Over 'Ouse and lives wiv the proper rogues like coney-catchers 'n jackmen. Us 'ere in Nether 'Ouse is only kynchin morts 'n kynchin coves 'n nippers 'n foisters 'n fraters 'n walking morts 'n dommerers 'n—"

Linnet, almost completely unenlightened except for the vague impression that Over House was for greater knaves than Nether House, said so. Nan verified this, after much patient prodding. A prigger, it seemed, was a thief, a dommerer a spurious deaf-mute, a frater someone begging with a forged license. Nan herself, she confessed sadly, was only a frater, being too stupid for anything else. But she had a beautiful forged license. She took the tin token from her scrawny bosom for Linnet to see.

" 'N all these little 'n's is kynchin morts and kynchin coves," she added, from which the shocked Linnet gathered that they were apprentices to a life of higher crime, all being ambitious to move upward on that ladder.

"Does Colley just ride around the highways of England looking for stray children?" she demanded, as a sudden horrifying suspicion struck.

But Nan shook her head. "Only yer, 'n that was 'cos 'e needed a flash dell—a gentry mort, I mean—for a plan 'e's got. I 'eard 'im telling Maudlin. The rest of us is mostly orphans wot would've died in the street if 'e 'adn't took us in." Her face shone with gratitude. " 'E gives us a place ter live, 'n food 'n clothes 'n blankets, 'n 'e teaches us trades, 'n only lets us do the work us is fit ter do, so us 'ardly ever ends up on the nubbing cheat."

"What's the nubbing cheat?" asked the fascinated Linnet, hardly able to believe her ears.

"Gallows," said Nan, surprised.

Linnet shivered suddenly, not entirely from cold. Nan thought the matter over. "Glad I 'aven't the wits ter prig," she decided comfortably. "Beggin's safer, even if I don't never get to Over 'Ouse." It was clear that begging was the lowest rung of the social ladder here, merely tolerated by self-respecting rogues. Linnet didn't care to think too deeply about the upper rungs. . . . She shivered again.

6

Dead Ends

Despite all Linnet's indignant protests, Colley left her to settle herself into Nether House—under Maudlin's dour eyes, and with the constant guardianship of Nan and a hulking fellow named Alfie who sat stolidly by the front door with one thought firmly fixed in his small and sluggish brain. Linnet wasn't to go out. No matter what. It might have been awkward indeed had the house caught fire. . . .

Nan was prepared to be humble, sociable, and informative. "Colley picked us ter stay wiv yer acause we'm not much use outside any'ow," she explained cheerfully. "Too big 'n too ugly ter move people's 'earts begging, 'n too stupid ter do anyfing else."

Linnet could readily see this. Alfie, in fact, reminded her strongly of faithful old Jemmy at home. Both were large and shambling, both had faces that looked as if several armies had absent-mindedly marched across them, and both wore expressions of amiable imbecility. Linnet might almost have warmed to Alfie for that reason—except that Jemmy was a faithful servant and Alfie was a minion of Colley, whom she had now decided to regard as an enemy. She gave poor Alfie a look of such concentrated ferocity that it penetrated even that insensitive perception and put a bewildered pucker on his pasty face. The new dell seemed to be angered at him for some reason, and he couldn't think why. He was quite sure he hadn't hit her or anything. Colley had said not to. And what else could anyone possibly be angered about?

Nan understood perfectly that such a lady resented having to associate with the lower orders. She didn't blame her a bit. "I won't touch yer," she promised apologetically. "I'll even bring in some water if yer wants to wash," she added doubtfully. " 'N Maudlin says us is ter throw out the slops."

"To what?" Linnet stared incredulously.

"Empty the slops," repeated Nan, even more apologetically.

"Well, I shan't!" Linnet informed her flatly. Nothing could induce her to do any such thing. Slops, indeed! Her stomach revolted at the thought.

"Ar, I thought yer wouldn't," said Nan without surprise. " 'S all right; I'll do it. But could yer come too, please? If I lets yer out o' my sight, I'll get a beating, 'n me back's still sore from the last. Yer needn't get too close; just not ter let Maudlin know yer ain't 'elping."

"Oh, all right," said Linnet ungraciously. She wished Nan didn't somehow make her feel so uncomfortable and guilty—as if she were in the habit of kicking dogs or something. Sullenly she followed Nan upstairs and waited as she carried the reeking buckets one by one to the nearest window, bawled "Slops!" at the top of her voice, and emptied them briskly into the streets. On the last one, a yell from below suggested that someone hadn't jumped in time. Nan giggled.

Linnet frowned thoughtfully. Surely, now she came to think of it, this was an unsatisfactory method of doing things. Couldn't some clever person like Father invent a better one? Like—oh, like a hole in the ground under each house—or something.

She found herself staring at Nan curiously as the taller girl led the way downstairs. What did it feel like to be a —well, a Nan? Did the lower orders like being lower orders? Did they care? Did they really have not much more sensibility than dogs or horses? What did the world look like through Nan's eyes? It was the first time Linnet had ever wondered such a novel thing, but now she had wondered it, she could not let it go.

"What would you like to do, Nan, if you could do any-thing in the world?" she demanded.

Nan, whose faculty of imagination had been totally un-developed, gaped. She found the very idea bewildering.

"If you could be or do anything," Linnet repeated.

"But I can't," Nan explained simply. "I'm Nan. Can't be nubbody else, can't do nothin' else."

It was no more than Linnet had expected, but it aroused all her obstinacy. "Well, just pretend," she urged. "Sup-pose a fairy came and gave you a wish. Would you want money? Would you like to be clever and go to Over House? Or be a fine lady in lovely clothes? Or what?"

Nan struggled. These last two suggestions were quite beyond her scope, but there was something. . . . "I'd like ter go outside the town walls every day," she confessed. "I likes the grass 'n green fings, 'n flowers. If I was clever, see, Colley'd use me for a maid in a big 'ouse outside Lunnen ter spy for 'im, 'n nose out Papist plots 'n all, 'n then I c'd see green meadows 'n fine people all the time." She sighed, quite carried away by this unusual flight of fancy. Then she peered anxiously at Linnet, just in case she had some-how offended her.

In fact, she had, in a way. Linnet was feeling uncomfort-able again, and it was a most offensive feeling, especially on top of her annoyances and worries. After all, she was the injured and aggrieved one, wasn't she? Being kept here, a virtual prisoner. . . . Plot or no plot, it was wrong of Colley!

But before she could do more than turn that annoyed waggling right eyebrow upon Nan, there was the inevi-table noisy screech of the front door opening, a thud of someone crashing against Alfie, and a duet of swearing in treble and baritone. This was followed by a loud roar, and the roar was followed by Peace.

"I want 'im!" she bawled, erupting into the common room and charging toward the fireplace and the ever-sim-mering pot. " 'E's mine. I saved 'im; this time I saved 'im, Maudlin, and nubbody can't kill 'im, 'n you can make 'im all well again, 'n 's all right, innit?"

She skidded to a halt in front of Maudlin and shoved at her a small matted bundle she had been clutching to her chest. Her pointy little face was ablaze. She was a perfectly terrifying child, clearly capable of any kind of wickedness and violence.

Maudlin seemed unterrified. She glanced at the furry bundle, poked it, shrugged. "Dead," she said. "Good thing,

50

too. You know you can't 'ave no cat to live 'ere; you been told that. Kynchin coves 'd kill it. Throw it away 'n go back to work, or I'll tell Colley."

Peace hugged the disgusting corpse to her chest, stamped, and roared like a dozen lions from the Tower of London. Enormous tears poured down her face in an amazing flow. Between roars she bawled at the top of her lungs that it mustn't be dead, she'd saved it from the 'prentices, she wanted to keep it to sleep with her, and if she couldn't have this, she'd find another.

In the middle of the uproar, Colley appeared as if by magic. Peace turned on him defiantly and went through the whole scene all over again, while Linnet stared in fascination. Eventually Colley took the dead cat, and gave it to Maudlin for disposal. Peace yelled and kicked at him with a small bare foot. Colley turned her over and smacked her bare thigh where it appeared through the rags. Then he shook her, picked her up in surprisingly gentle arms, and stared her into silence. After which he set her down, patted her drenched cheek, and told her to run along and do some good begging while she still looked so pitiable and tragic.

Peace obeyed, meekly enough. But her face had a certain look of stubborn determination that didn't escape Linnet's eyes, even though it was turned away from Colley.

Colley turned, saw Linnet, and nodded cheerfully. He was dressed as a rich merchant today, in plum and blue; and his conscience (if he had one, which was beginning to seem extremely doubtful) was perfectly at ease regarding his prisoner. One might think he had done her a favor in letting her stay here.

"Silly poppet," he observed in the direction of the squeal and thud of the front door. "She has an idiot notion that she can find a stray cat and keep it as a pet, the way the gentry do. Still, she's a clever child. I'll have you teach her fine speech and manners one of these days; it might come in handy."

"No!" said Linnet automatically but without much conviction.

Colley rightly ignored this as a rather pathetic bit of bravado, and went on as if she hadn't opened her mouth. "I'll take you out tomorrow and show you a bit of London," he said. "Nan, you can outfit her, and if you fumble it, I'll skin you."

Nan didn't look particularly scared. "I'll get 'er in prime twig," she promised, all enthusiasm. "Cap downright if I don't!"

"You'd better," he said carelessly. "Useless baggage that you are, I'll turn you out one of these days if you don't start showing a profit."

It seemed an odd kind of threat to Linnet, who could think of nothing she'd like better. But Nan turned quite white and went on her knees, babbling that she'd do better, truly she would, and please please let her stay.

"Well, you can turn me out just any time, and I shan't be the least bit upset," Linnet offered acidly.

Colley laughed. "You'd change your mind in about ten minutes, Sparrow. Besides, I wouldn't turn you out for the world. Think of the Queen! Now run up with Nan to the wardrobe room and look over what you're to wear tomorrow. I'll drop back tonight to see you."

"But why?" demanded Linnet. "What's all this to do

with the plot? Why can't we just go and—and do whatever it is, like telling Sir Francis Walsingham, which I don't see why you didn't do in the first place. After all, he is the Secretary of State and everyone knows he tries to discover plots against the Queen."

"My dear Sparrow, 'tis not nearly that simple, I assure you. Now do stop adding to my difficulties, and go do as I say."

Linnet obeyed, seething. A quarter of an hour later, in the middle of a pile of wildly assorted garments, she suddenly frowned, lifted her head, sat back on her heels, and began thinking deeply.

"Wot's the matter?" asked Nan anxiously. "Wot yer doin'?"

"Thinking," muttered Linnet.

Nan looked more anxious than ever. "You'll 'urt yourself," she warned uneasily.

Linnet ignored this. "Has Colley gone?" she demanded. Nan was sure he had. Why would he hang about? "Well, I didn't hear him go," Linnet reflected aloud. "And that door makes the most awful racket, so I should have heard it. And I didn't hear it when he came in, either."

"Peace was 'avin' 'er fit," Nan pointed out with simple logic. "Yer couldn't 'ave 'eard a 'ole mob. 'Ere, try this."

Linnet put on a filthy rag of a skirt, too abstracted to notice what it was like. "Well, yes; but I do think I should have heard him go out, because I was listening, and it was quiet. And if it comes to that, I didn't hear him come in last night."

Nan sat back on her own heels and thought about it. " 'Strewf," she discovered suddenly. " 'E don't never make no noise comin' or goin'. And I ain't 'ardly ever seed 'im come or go, 'e just appears. I think 'e does it by magic." And she began turning over clothing again, perfectly satisfied by this explanation.

"Black magic, I'll warrant," muttered Linnet, who was beginning to feel increasingly uncharitable toward him, Queen or no Queen. She could easily visualize him appearing and disappearing in puffs of sulphurous smoke. She fell to brooding. What if he *were* in league with the Devil? What if all that plausibility and charm were the snares of Satan? Panic gripped at her. If that were so, she was lost indeed, for it would need a great deal of divine intervention to help her, and Linnet was not at all certain she had much influence with heaven. The whole idea was so terrifying that she put it right out of her mind and forced her attention back to matters at hand.

"Ugh!" she said vehemently, looking at the skirt she was wearing, and began to take it off.

"Told you so," sighed Hugh, hoping that his friend was now prepared to be reasonable. For three days they had been tracking down and interviewing various Seymours in pursuit of Linnet, and the experience had not been rewarding.

Lord Hertford's two sons were civil, if only just. Preoccupied with their own affairs, they knew little about their father's cousin's daughter, and cared less. In fact, the only interest they showed in the whole matter was frank alarm at the possibility of Linnet showing up for Edward's wedding. If she did, they promised fervently, they would notify Lord Crowden at once!

Lord Hertford's sister Anne, now Lady Unton, said she was sorry to hear Tom and Robin had lost a daughter, but she didn't say it very convincingly. If anything, Giles decided, she was slightly pleased. One gathered that back in those childhood days in Henry VIII's Court, Anne had not been on very good terms with Tom and Robin.

Henry Seymour was at sea, and the others were either dead or living in remote places like Devon or Northamptonshire—except for the dowager Duchess of Somerset, of course. . . .

Giles thought twice about seeing Lady Somerset, even though she was Linnet's father's uncle's wife, and therefore Linnet's great-aunt. There was no love lost there, he was fairly sure, and everyone who knew her agreed that the lady was probably the most vicious, rapacious, and unscrupulous female alive. It seemed highly unlikely that Linnet would have sought refuge there, except as a last resort . . . but Giles was determined not to miss a possibility.

"You wouldn't!" said Hugh, horrified.

"Yes I would," retorted Giles, and went.

She was indeed a perfectly beastly old lady, married now to her dead husband's ex-steward. Giles felt sure she was perfectly capable of flinging Linnet into a dungeon on sight, just to spite Linnet's parents, whom Lady Somerset clearly hated with great venom. But the browbeaten footman who ushered the boys hastily out (pursued by a storm of very unladylike abuse) whispered that no red-headed little girl had been near the place.

"Whew!" remarked Giles when they stood again in the street, the door firmly closed against them. "I'm glad she didn't come here, anyway!"

"She didn't come to London at all," insisted Hugh, still thinking of his new falcon and how much more fun it would be to go hawking. "I told you so all along. Do listen to reason, Giles."

Giles consulted his intuition again and found it implacable. "Yes she did," he said with decision. "And what's more, I'm going to find her."

Hugh looked startled. "Find her?" he bleated, pained. "My poor clod-poll, how on earth do you expect to do that? If she's just loose in London—" He shrugged eloquently.

Giles looked at him. "I'll just look until I do," he announced with staggering simplicity.

Hugh stopped short in the middle of the Strand. "You can't mean it!" he begged, knowing perfectly well that Giles did mean it. "Oh, well." He looked martyred. "I suppose I shall have to help, even though I've never even seen the little minx. Can't think why you want to find her, anyway; you'd be far better off without her. I'll find you a pretty little flirt like Amy. We'll be old men with beards, and still hunting," he prophesied pathetically. "I know you, Giles!" He sighed heavily. "When do we start? How about next Monday?"

"This minute," said Giles, just as Hugh had known he would. "Come on."

7

London Streets

"Yer looks jus' like a fine lady dressed up as a beggar," said Nan discontentedly and with surprising acumen.

This did not at all surprise Linnet, who felt just like a fine lady dressed up as a beggar. She looked with revulsion at the assortment of once-bright rags held together largely by encrusted dirt. From it, her pixie face, still relatively clean, emerged like a water lily from a pool of stagnant sludge.

"Somefing ain't just right," Nan decided, sounding pleased with herself for having figured the thing out alone. "We'll ask Colley." And she led the way down the dark twisty stairs.

It was a stormy night, wind and rain howling around corners and through the narrow mazelike streets of London and in at every chink of Nether House. A fierce rattling sound from down the street suggested that the Sign of the Pied Bull was earnestly trying to pull itself off its hinges and attack the Happy Cockerel just beyond, and that the Happy Cockerel was in turn trying to escape. Linnet shivered and wondered what it was like here in winter, and hoped most passionately that she would never find out.

In the common room below, everyone had got home from work wet and cold, and were gratefully but quarrelsomely drying out around the stingy fire in the huge fireplace. It was, explained Nan, never built up for more than cooking in the summer. Think of all the wasted fuel! Maudlin was stirring the eternal pease porridge in the pot. There was a pile of coarse black maslin bread and old cheese on the trestled table.

Linnet, perfectly aware of her own superiority, was wearing her usual scowl of revulsion at everything about Nether House. Disgusting place and people! She seated herself aloofly on the hard bench, amid a small tight silence. The others stared back at her with resentment.

This was slightly surprising to Linnet, who would have expected all of them to share Nan's attitude of anxious-to-please reverence. Her eyebrow jutted out arrogantly, and she contrived to look even haughtier than before.

This had an effect, but not the desired one. Salamon spat in her direction. The buxom, darkly-pretty girl named Joan placed fists on hips, stuck her chin in the air, and minced across the floor in an unmistakable and highly unflattering caricature that was thought tremendously funny by everyone but Linnet, who carefully failed to perceive it. Several brats in the corner whispered and giggled, the older girls snickered maliciously, and Peace erupted directly in front of Linnet.

"Talk!" she commanded deafeningly. "Yer talks funny, like a lady, 'n Colley says I'm ter learn 'ow."

Linnet at once forgot to be haughty and aloof. She bent a critical eye upon the scrawny scrap. "Well, I don't think it would be the least use your trying," she pronounced judiciously. "I mean, you can't just go around changing your accent, little goose."

This was met by a derisive hoot and a suggestion that she listen to Colley switch accents some time. And as if conjured up by the mention of his name, Colley was there again, sauntering through from that maze of corridors leading to the front door. Had its squeak and thud been drowned out by the noise? Or—? Linnet sniffed the air for a hint of sulphur fumes, but the other stenches made it impossible to tell.

He laughed when he saw her in rags. "Can't make a sow's ear out of a silk purse quite so easily, can we?" he chuckled, to the vast confusion of Alfie, who had followed him in. Alfie had been very much puzzled anyway, as to whether this new bird was a linnet or a sparrow. Now it seemed she was either a silk purse or a sow's ear. She didn't look much like any of them. He peered at her, bewildered.

"I didn't see no silk purses, not in the wardrobe boxes," said Nan apologetically. "I'm sorry, Colley; wot did I do wrong?"

Colley boxed her ear good-naturedly. "Witling," he said. "You should have known she'd never pass as a beggar, even if I wanted another. Now go back up and dress her as a shopkeeper's daughter, little noddle-skull, before I slit your sneezer."

Nan scuttled upstairs, pulling the protesting Linnet with her.

When they appeared again, Colley looked mildly approving. "Not bad," he conceded. "Aye, well enough. I'll take you on a tour of London in that, Sparrow; perhaps tomorrow. I think we'll cover your hair, though. 'Tis too well tended for anyone but a gentry mort—but perfect for your role in our counterplot." Linnet pricked up her ears at this hint, and waited hopefully for another, but he was apparently lost in admiration of the luxuriant copper curls hanging down her back. Hair was a maiden's pride and respectability, flowing loose until after her marriage. Linnet's own was her particular joy, almost making up for the unfortunate freckles on her nose, for it really was of a lovely color and shine and softness, besides being fashionable and like Queen Elizabeth. She endured his inspection with frank complacency that caused Joan's eyes to narrow.

"Wigmaker'd pay a mort for that 'air," she suggested. "Red, too. All the style."

Linnet backed away a step, clutching it protectively. The kynchin morts giggled and the kynchin coves grinned. Colley chuckled amiably.

"Wouldn't like to lose it, eh, Sparrow?"

"Of course not," said Linnet with dignity. "No respectable girl would have short hair, would she? Besides, mine's my only beauty, so I particularly want to keep it." And then she bit her unruly tongue. Why did she always blurt out whatever she was thinking? The morts were giggling again, delighted at such an admission.

Colley studied her with a judicious air. "Nay, now," he decided. "Who told you that? Giles? 'Tis true you've that very peculiar eyebrow, and freckles, and too much mouth. But you've also nice white teeth, which is a rare enough thing, and a saucy nose if not a dignified one, and green eyes that any mort would envy." (The morts tossed their heads pettishly and denied this.) "Anyway," Colley went on with a chuckle, "you're wrong about no nice girl having short hair, isn't she, Joan?"

Joan, grinning, unwrapped a bundle she had placed on the table when she came in. "There's plenty in London do," she pointed out, displaying a mass of long, fair, silky hair. "You shoulda 'eard 'er yell! Bit me fumb, 'er did." She nursed the thumb.

Colley laughed again at Linnet's expression. "Lures little girls into dark alleys, Joan does, and cuts off their hair. Wigmakers pay well. Be good, Sparrow, or I'll let her have yours."

But this time Linnet failed to show alarm. She had just thought of something.

"Well, you won't," she told him. "You need my hair on me for whatever it is I'm to do for the Queen. You just said so."

She tilted her head at Colley, who looked faintly startled and then amused. "Astute Sparrow," he said, and tousled the hair.

The tall shopkeeper emerged from the narrow house in Slops Alley, hurried past the Pied Bull and Happy Cockerel, and headed straight for a more respectable street. He led his young daughter by the hand, glancing down at her now and then with a look of paternal affection. Clearly a most devoted father! Linnet dimpled back at him, quite forgetting her annoyance about housing conditions. At last she was seeing London!

It was a dozen worlds! It was a jewel, a cesspool, a mob,

and a fair! Linnet felt crowded into her own eyes and ears, staring avidly, loving even the bits she loathed. And to think that Mother and Father deliberately chose to live in the empty countryside instead!

They paced along narrow, crooked streets, bright with swinging shop signs, houses staggering any which way. Upper stories pushed farther and farther outwards until they nearly met overhead and only a strip of sky came shining through—just above the strip of reeking gutter along the center of every cobbled street. They saw the craft streets: Ironmonger Lane and Silver Street, Milk Street and Bread Street (smelling deliciously of new-baked loaves), Cordwainer Street and Distaff Lane, each devoted to its own guild. There was noise like the surge of ocean: of hammers and ringing anvils, shouts and quarrels of apprentices always eager for battle with some rival guild, cries of vendors, a muffin man and a fishmonger and a flower woman, the laughter and squeals of children. There were flowerpots of gay blooms in windows, and filth in the gutters. There were strolling players, morris dancers, a performing bear led by a little boy, wandering fiddlers and a ballad-monger. There were lords on horseback, a lady in a litter with servants running ahead to clear the way, merchants in furred gowns, and scabby, wheedling beggars and fortune-tellers—several of whom Linnet recognized.

There was Billingsgate, the fish market, with its stalls piled high with silver-scaled wares, and the scurrying, swearing world of its dockland, and russet sails of fishing smacks and oyster boats against the shimmer of the Thames; tiltboats with painted gunwales and shouting, singing watermen, and a glimpse of a lord's pleasure barge just going under the crowded pile of houses that was London Bridge.

There were other streets and sights, too, which would haunt Linnet until the day she died. What a mercy it was that the lower classes had dull senses and minds. It was to be hoped, she reflected, that their senses and minds were a good deal duller than those of the dogs and horses at Fontenay, since their living conditions were so much worse. . . .

And here and there were more glimpses of Colley's Flock, begging or wandering among crowds with expressions of shattering innocence—especially in the wide market street Chepeside, where fat purses and the tempting stalls all down the center offered irresistible opportunities for dishonesty.

Linnet took it all in tirelessly for hours. Then she turned a suddenly inquiring face up to Colley's. "I'm confused," she complained. "Why don't you ever explain anything?"

"What do you need explained?" he asked benevolently.

"Well, everything, but especially why I have to stay in Nether House, and about the plot. Who's plotting it, and what are they plotting, and when, and how am I supposed to help, and why me instead of anyone else; and if you never have time to explain any of these things to me, how is it that you have time to take a whole day and show me London?"

He smiled down at her. "Don't you think it's important that you see London?"

Linnet knitted her eyebrows. "Well, of course I think

it's important, because that's why I came to London in the first place, isn't it? But I shouldn't think you'd think it very important."

"You wrong me, Sparrow," protested Colley, looking injured. "Don't you think I care about your happiness?"

Linnet surprised herself. "Well, no," she discovered. "Not really. Because if you did, you wouldn't make me stay in Nether House, for one thing. You use people, and belike you only care about me being useful to you, and you're just showing me London so I'll forget to mind about all the other things." She cocked her head to peer at his face with interest. It was a most astonishing conclusion she had just reached, and she wanted to see if he was going to be very angry.

"Sparrow!" he exclaimed, his eyes soft with reproach. "Do you truly think so ill of me?"

"Well—" Linnet at once began to melt. "You act that way," she pointed out, but with diminishing conviction.

"You mustn't judge people by appearances," Colley told her severely.

Linnet rallied. "Well, I know I shouldn't, because if I hadn't, I should never have thought you were a gentleman, would I? And then I wouldn't have been hit on the head and made to go live with the fleas and lice and the lower orders. Because you appeared to be a perfect gentleman, and it was only afterwards I found out you're a knave and a rogue and the Upright Man." She jerked her pointed chin at him in triumph, and tried to look quelling, but it was impossible with him grinning at her so mischievously.

"A touch, Sparrow. But then, if you hadn't trusted me,

you'd never have been able to help me save the Queen, would you?"

Linnet suddenly perceived that she had been sidetracked off that very subject some moments earlier. "Yes, well that reminds me, you still haven't answered any of my questions, have you? So far, I haven't done a single thing to help, and I don't even know anything about it, and don't you think we ought to hurry? What if they go ahead and assassinate her or invade England or whatever it is they're planning, while we're just sitting around in Nether House or even seeing London?"

"All in good time," he said soothingly. "Don't fret, poppet. No, no more now. Come, here's St. Paul's ahead. You'll want to see it, and I've some business there."

"In a cathedral?" Linnet demanded, sidetracked again. Colley didn't strike her as being at all a religious man. "What kind of business could you have there?"

"Any kind you can think of." He tousled her hair again, making her feel rather like a puppy having its ears rumpled. "Come see."

Linnet stared at the sharp spire which dominated the sky between rooftops, and now loomed imposingly over the open area of Chepe. She stared even harder when they got inside, and with a strong sense of shock. St. Paul's was a veritable marketplace. The nave—St. Paul's Walk, Colley called it—was lined on both sides with stalls, bookshops, and lawyers and scribes waiting to be hired. All were doing a thriving business. Here, said Colley, lovers and plotters met (Linnet pricked up her ears at that), business deals were arranged, quarrels arose and were settled, and fashionable men and women paraded up and down showing off their newest finery. And here Colley remained for a full hour, apparently doing a good bit of business.

But when he had finished, and they were starting home, Linnet returned to a certain subject with a tenacity that surprised Colley.

" 'Tis all very well to say all in good time, but that doesn't prove a thing, does it? Besides, I haven't got much time. I can't just stay here forever and ever, you know, because if I do, someone's going to notice that I'm not in Guildford or at home, and get their tails in knots." She sighed a little, thinking of Giles. Adventure lacked savor without him; she must arrange in the future not to exclude him so thoroughly.

"I'm not delaying matters just to annoy you, Sparrow," said Colley reasonably. "The fact is, we can't do anything until a certain family returns to London. When that day comes. . . . Believe me, Sparrow, I'm as eager as you."

"Oh," said Linnet, and had to be satisfied.

"I thought I saw her," said Ned. "I mean, it might have been. 'Twas at St. Paul's. But then I thought not, for the maid was wearing common clothing, and with a common merchant, and perfectly at ease with him, too. But when I wanted a closer look, I lost her in the crowd, and couldn't see her again, though I stayed and searched—until I had my purse cut," he finished despondently.

Giles looked fiercely determined. "Good, Ned. I think we'll try to keep you or Wat or me watching at St. Paul's entrance every day, just in case. 'Tis a good center, anyway. Hugh—"

"Marry, I'm no use," said Hugh hastily. "Don't know the girl; never saw her in my life."

"Aye," Giles conceded regretfully. "Oh well. But I do think 'tis a pity, that."

"I don't," said Hugh with relief.

8

The Plot

And after that lovely day of sightseeing, Colley apparently forgot she existed, and left her to sulk for the next two days in Nether House, with nothing to do, and only the disgusting company of its inhabitants. Moreover, Maudlin glared and Alfie guarded the door and Nan quite literally hovered. As if they had been prison warders, under orders to prevent her from leaving in case she changed her mind about helping with the counterplot.

Linnet considered this. She was developing a nasty suspicious mind these days, and at least half the time she wasn't at all sure she trusted Colley, after all; and now and then she was sure of it. Moreover, she reflected, fuming, he didn't trust her, either. How dare he treat her like this? He really was a cullionly caitiff!

When he appeared on the second night, silently as usual, she greeted him with a scowl and a jutting lip.

"How, now," he said, arms akimbo. " 'Tis a bear instead of a sparrow tonight, I see. Shall I set my dogs on you?"

"I dare you!" retorted Linnet, eyes green and dangerous.

Peace, who never needed much excuse to start a brawl, at once began to bark and growl, and rushed at Linnet like a miniature bulldog. Linnet, to her own surprise, forgot her dignity and that she was not associating with any of Nether House. She turned herself into a bear, and threw both forepaws around Peace in a distinctly aggressive hug.

Peace instantly erupted into an awesome combination of mad dog, Bedlamite, and shrieking fiend from hell; and it was not at all certain whether this was in fun or not. Linnet, on the whole, felt not—and also began to think that she was no match at all for this small devil who had spent the whole of her short life fighting for existence. The whole thing was rapidly degenerating into a fight to the death, and one which Linnet was by no means sure of winning, when Colley plucked Peace off.

"You mustn't kill each other yet," he told them good-naturedly. "I need you both. Time for pocket practice, goslings. You first, Peace, and if you ring a bell I'll box your ears. Want to try it, Sparrow?"

Linnet bristled. "Me? Try thieving? How dare you? You ought to be ashamed of yourself, training children to steal, even if you are loyal to the Queen." She addressed herself to the Flock. "Don't you know it's dishonest? You really are very bad, you know."

They stared at her, puzzled and resentful. What was she talking about? Joan, who was undisputed leader of the kynchin morts, glared and spat. Salamon bristled.

"We ain't!" he declared, insulted. "Colley don't train no bad prigs. 'E don't let us prig 'nless us is good at it."

"Well, I don't mean bad that way," snapped Linnet, deeply annoyed at what seemed to be a kind of ethical idiocy in Nether House. "I mean, 'tis wicked to steal. You'll go to hell."

No one seemed deeply moved by this prediction.

"Same thing any road," Diggory explained with a philosophical shrug of his wide but bony shoulders. "Go sooner if we cocks up our toes wiv 'unger." But they went on looking puzzled. Why was the gentry mort attacking their profession this way? It didn't hurt her, surely?

"Tell you wot 'tis," Joan growled, coming forward to glare at Linnet while Colley stood back watching with an expression of amused interest. "You gentry 'ave things all your own way, don't you? Your pockets and bellies is full; you got everything 'n we got nothing, so you makes rules saying we can't 'ave nothing or 'tis wicked 'n you'll 'ang us."

"No such thing!" cried Linnet indignantly. " 'Tis only that you mustn't steal it."

" 'Ow else d'you think we could get it?" Joan demanded.

"Well—earn it, of course," said Linnet, but a trifle doubtfully. Joan favored her with a contemptuous laugh and turned away. The pocket practice went on as if nothing had happened, leaving Linnet to smolder upon her hard bench. She could not feel that she had entirely won the argument.

"Welladay," said Colley presently. "Keep it up, then, goslings. Joan and Peace, you'll be promoted one day soon, if you continue to please me. Give ye good night. Come along, Sparrow." And he started for the door.

"No," muttered Linnet. Then, since he didn't come back or argue with her, or even pause, she was forced to back down. "Oh, very well," she cried, and scuttled after him with far more haste than dignity. She was not going to miss any chance to escape Nether House! Besides, it occurred to her that Colley had once more appeared without a sound from the clamorous front door, and if he was about to disappear in a cloud of sulphur, Linnet very much wanted to see it.

Alas, he did no such thing, but walked out in the most ordinary way. The door groaned and banged behind them, and Linnet hurried in the golden evening sunshine to catch up.

"Where are we going?" she demanded. "Is it the counterplot now? What am I supposed to do? You might at least tell me something," she added plaintively.

"Wait and see," he returned infuriatingly, and proceeded to lead her on a most torturous course, turning nearly every corner they came to, twisting through narrow stinking alleys and wider streets that seemed respectable only by comparison. Linnet, who happened to have a natural sense of direction, began to frown thoughtfully. She opened her mouth to tell Colley that they were going in circles, and this was the second time they had passed this corner where one could just glimpse the Happy Cockerel and the entrance to Slops Alley down the side street, and if he was lost, he had best ask directions. Then it occurred to her that Colley knew every foot of London as well as she knew Fontenay. So—he must be going in circles on purpose!

Linnet was developing an extremely suspicious mind. The misanthropic idea came to her that if he were doing it on purpose, it might well be with a mind to deceiving her.

She opened her mouth to inform him of this, and then closed it for the second time. If he were doing it to deceive her, he clearly knew it already, and it might be more clever of her not to tell him that she knew.

"Why do you always have to make such a mystery of everything?" she demanded. "Why can't you just tell me where—oh!" She peered through the fading sunset—for it was now after eight of the clock—at the high wall ahead. "Isn't this Over House, where I came the first night and your horrid Gregory hit me on the head? Because I have a few things I want to say to him, even if he was obeying your orders. And why couldn't you have told me we were coming here, to begin with?"

"Stubble it, Sparrow," said Colley rather absent-mindedly, and led the way in.

Linnet had never found it possible to stay angry in the face of affability. And Colley was decidedly affable that evening. He turned her over to Kitty, who whisked her off for a good hot bath that very nearly caused Linnet to forgive everything on the spot.

"I only come up from Nether 'Ouse—I mean House —at Easter," Kitty confided over soap and scrub brush. "Colley's training me ter be a lady's maid, and 'e says I must listen to 'ow you talk and copy it. Ain't 'e wonderful?"

"Well—he's very surprising," Linnet conceded cautiously, not quite ready to go as far as Kitty in the matter. "Now let's wash my hair."

"Your 'air?" Kitty looked shocked. She was slowly getting used to the ways of gentry and the occasional use of soap, but a bath every six months or so was, she felt, quite radical enough. Surely washing hair was unnatural?

"Dunno if Colley'd like it," she demurred.

"Who cares if he does or not?" asked Linnet in surprise. " 'Tis nothing to do with him. Except that it's his fault I've got bugs in it." And she dunked her head into the hot water to preclude all argument.

Kitty, darkly predicting almost instant death of a rheum or worse, gave in, helped soap it, and spent a full hour brushing it dry. After which she looked at the silken waves gleaming exactly the color of copper in the soft candle-light, and conceded it looked wondrous pretty, at that.

"Well, that's why I wash it much oftener than I should," Linnet confided sleepily. "Because it feels lovely and it looks nice. When it's dirty, 'tis just a dull pinkish-red and Giles says rude things about it." She looked at the big four-poster bed with embroidered curtains hung around it. "I notice Colley didn't say anything this time about it not being proper for me to sleep here," she observed with triumph. " 'Tis what I've thought all along: he just arranges his notions of right and wrong to suit his convenience."

"Aye, to be sure," agreed Kitty, surprised. "Doesn't everybody?"

Linnet saw Colley at dinner the next morning, which they had at the fashionable hour of ten. A proper dinner, she was delighted to see, and not just the dry-bread-and-pease-porridge breakfast that the Flock had before setting out on a day's begging, prigging, and general roguery. No doubt it was what the lower orders liked, she told Colley severely, helping herself to a little more salad and roast capon, but she herself liked a proper dinner in the morning, or even as late as noon.

"So I see," commented Colley dryly, watching her make inroads on the beef and mutton, stewed carp, and a side dish of boiled radish and artichoke.

Linnet favored him with a reproachful stare. "Well, when you think what I've been forced to eat lately—" she began in outraged tones.

Colley hastily handed her a bowl of boiled stringy stems of an astonishing shade of bright pink. "Here, try this," he urged. "Something from China called patience. Comes in thick pink stalks with huge leaves."

Mollified, Linnet forgot her grievance and tasted. Tart and sweet. She had another bowl, sighed happily, indignantly refused even the smallest sip of wine, remembered to glare at Gregory, and leaned back in her chair.

"If you'd treated me like this to begin with—I mean, to go on with," she told Colley, "we'd have got along much better. Now tell me about the plot and what I'm supposed to do to foil it and save Queen Bess, and let's hurry and do it so I can go home before Giles comes looking for me."

"Very well, then, listen carefully." He passed a bowl of sweet pears and oranges, and took one himself, addressing himself to the flattered Linnet as if she were a grown lady. "I have managed to become very friendly with some of our leading Papist families over these last months, and I'm sure there's something big afoot, involving the Spanish Ambassador Mendoza."

"And Mary of Scotland?" queried Linnet excitedly.

"Mary, of course," Colley agreed. "But I can't learn any more. These Papists take me into their homes, but not into their confidence. They have nasty distrustful minds, these plotters." He wagged his head sadly. "Seem to think Walsingham has government spies under every bed."

"Well, so he should, and I wish he did," declared Linnet roundly. It seemed an altogether reasonable precaution, considering the number of Papist plots already unearthed against the Queen.

"Mmm," said Colley obliquely. "Very like. But the point is, my dear friends the Throckmortons seem only to trust me so far and no further."

" 'Tis monstrous churlish of them!" cried Linnet, carried away.

"Aye," Colley agreed solemnly. "Most brutish. They act as if I might turn out to be a clever and plausible knave out to spy on them, or something."

Linnet stared, giggled suddenly, then frowned. "Well, but this time you're not *really* being a knave, because 'tis for the Queen," she pointed out.

"To be sure," Colley agreed at once. "No need to chafe, Sparrow. Now let me finish, do. In order to invoke more trust, I've allowed myself to be converted to the Roman faith by one of that army of Jesuit priests who have been swarming into England this past two or three years. Oh, no; not in sooth," he added hastily at Linnet's alarmed expression. "Only in pretense, Sparrow. It helped, but not enough. And it occurred to me that if I only had a family to be converted as well—particularly if it just happened to include a daughter of an age to be friends with young

75

Amy Throckmorton. . . . And behold, you appeared! My motherless daughter Jennet, living until recently with your aunt in—well, Wiltshire will do; 'tis large enough, and you really do know it, and the fewer inventions for you to remember, the better. So I shall bring you to visit them, and also to be converted. They won't be able to resist that, by my fay! In fact, they have just got back to London, and I've already informed them, and they're simply delighted with the prospect, quite prepared to take you under their wing and instruct you and let you play with Amy."

He regarded Linnet quizzically. She stared back, doubtful. "Do you mean you're going to pretend to be my father?" she demanded indignantly. "When you aren't even a gentleman?"

"Sir Colin Collyngewood of Collyngewood Hall," he reminded her with a low bow. "I fooled you, didn't I, Sparrow? And remember, if your pride thinks amiss of it, 'tis for the Queen," he added gently.

"Well, I know, but—" She considered it. "I can't pretend to be a Papist; I don't know anything about it."

"My dear Sparrow, you don't need to. You need know only that your dear father has been converted, and so you are prepared seriously to consider following his example. The more ignorant you are, the better, for your instruction can last that much longer and give us both that much more time in the company of the Throckmortons. Now for the love of all the saints, Sparrow, don't ask questions! Just keep your mouth shut and your ears open, and be as charming a young lady as you can. Become Amy's very best friend; do you understand? And it may just be that 'twill be you who hears the important little words let drop. D'you think you can do it? I count on you, my dear."

"Oh." Linnet felt pleased at this honor. "Well, of course I can. I just don't see why you waited so long—"

"My dear Sparrow, I've told you. The Throckmortons have been out of town."

"Oh, yes; I'd forgot." Linnet's mind was suddenly on something else. She narrowed her eyes at him so that her eyebrow pointed accusingly. "What's *your* lay?" she demanded disconcertingly in the thieves' cant she had been picking up in Nether House.

His own eyebrows soared, and he chuckled appreciatively. Then he looked reproachful. "My dear poppet, don't you think I'd serve our Queen from pure love and loyalty?"

She shook her bright head. "Well, no, I don't."

He nodded, not at all put out. "Quite right, too. I'm a businessman, and I see you're beginning to develop a more practical train of mind, yourself. Welladay, since you've bubbled my lay—aye, Sparrow, I intend to make a profit. Why not? I'm spending my time and trouble and brains; why shouldn't I be paid for it? And Walsingham rewards well for true evidence on such matters, and we're all better off save the plotters. So you see, I can combine virtue and profit." He cocked his pointed beard. "D'you think I should do it for love alone?"

"Well, yes, but I don't think you would." Linnet reached for another pear, feeling suddenly very old and wise in human nature. "In fact, if you hadn't told me about the reward, I daresay I should have thought you were up to something else, vile and devilish. For I don't believe you would lift a finger for anyone, not even Queen Elizabeth, unless you were paid for it." She reflected for a moment. "Still, so long as you confound the plot, I don't suppose I care why you do it or even how you do it, so I'll help as much as I can. And you needn't even pay me a share of the reward," she added generously.

"I wasn't going to," said Colley.

9

Counterplotting

"This is my daughter Jennet, Mistress Throckmorton. Jennet, make your curtsey."

Linnet did so, and her hostess took one comprehensive look and was pleased. Not that one doubted the charming Sir Colin, of course—but it was always better to know something of a friend's family. One could tell a lot that way. And there was no question at all of young Jennet's quality. It showed in every word and gesture. What a privilege to help save such a nice child from heresy and damnation, not to mention the unfortunate consequences for heretics when the Holy Father should at last rule again over England!

Mistress Throckmorton warmed perceptibly toward Sir Colin and his daughter at the thought. One learned to value true friends these days, when that wretched spymaster Walsingham had his spies planted everywhere, and was urging the Queen to permit repressive measures against Roman Catholics. And though she had not yet done so, she might at any moment. It made life exceedingly trying. . . .

"Amy will be down presently, sweeting," she told Linnet kindly, with another approving glance at the marks of breeding: the straight back and high head and glossy hair, and above all the self-confidence that came from knowing oneself superior. "There's a dish of sugared violets on the cabinet over there."

Linnet took one and seated herself demurely on a stool, savoring the pleasant feel of her own lacy petticoats and shoes once more. And Colley had produced for her a pair of pale green hosen, of real silk, like the Queen herself wore, and a dress as well. She smoothed the soft folds, approving the green embroidered leaves on the creamy petticoat that showed in an inverted V in front, and also the pale green and blue of the shot-taffeta bodice and overskirts.

Everything was all right at last. She could do her bit to uncover this newest plot on the Queen's life, and go on living at Over House in a civilized manner, and never again have anything to do with rags or pease porridge or any of the Flock, or anything at all connected with Nether House. And, who knew, she might yet finish her task and go home a heroine before anyone had time to notice she was missing. She smiled happily.

"My husband and Cousin Francis will be back anon," Mistress Throckmorton was saying. "You'll tarry, of course, for they—oh, here's Amy. This is Jennet Collyngewood, poppet; do you girls run into the garden and get acquainted."

Linnet followed the pale curls and violet skirts with very mixed feelings; elation and apprehension and determination in equal parts. It was exciting, playing the role of someone else, a mythical Jennet; and doubly satisfying because she was doing it for the Queen. On the other hand, there might be difficulties. . . .

The two girls turned to face each other in the middle of the garden, with searching eyes, not uncritical. It was at once clear to both of them that neither would really have chosen the other as a best friend. In fact, it soon began to appear to Linnet that they were so alien that they might well have belonged to two separate species, like the upper and lower classes, each unable to imagine how the other thought.

Amy was sleek and plump and bland and self-satisfied. Her pale hair and round pink-and-white prettiness suited her disposition very well, and she chattered in a way that made Linnet wonder uncomfortably whether her own conversation could possibly be as irritating. No, surely not! Amy was going on and on about new clothes and styles, and the Court functions she would attend as soon as she was old enough, and the young men who paid her compliments, and one Hugh in particular whose father was a Lord and who was heels over head in love with her, and what was the latest scandal in Court circles.

She found Linnet ignorant on all these subjects, and very dull. Linnet reflected with private satisfaction that she knew one young man, at least, who would simply loathe Amy and decline to pay her a single compliment—and she wished suddenly that he were here to do it right now. Amy fell silent at last, and the two girls looked at each other again, this time with mutual frustration.

"Mother says you're going to be converted to the True Faith like your father," said Amy at last in the condescending voice of one who was born in it.

Linnet controlled her wayward tongue just in time. Appalled at how nearly she had given her feelings away, she swallowed hard and stammered a little. "I—well—yes."

"That's good." Amy looked smug. "Then perhaps you won't be burnt for a heretic when Queen Mary—" She stopped, clapped a cluster of white fingers over her mouth, and turned pink. "I mean, perhaps you won't go to hell when you die."

Linnet's heart gave an odd sort of thump, and she stared at Amy, almost incredulous. It was what she had hoped and intended, of course, but—but she could hardly believe her ears, all the same. How could anyone, even a flaxen-curled fool, really say such a thing, or even think it?

"Why are you looking at me like that?" Amy demanded, uneasiness making her petulant. "What are you thinking?"

Taken by surprise, Linnet told her. "I was thinking how silly you are to say such things," she replied. "Especially to someone you've only just met and who isn't even converted yet. I mean, you don't know if I'm on your side at all, do you? And you don't know who I might tell."

"There's nothing to tell!" bleated Amy, thoroughly alarmed. "I didn't say anything, and anyway, you wouldn't tell, would you? Father'd be furious! I'm not supposed to know a thing about it, of course, and anyhow, all I said was what everybody knows, that Queen Mary should be on the throne because Elizabeth is a bastard and excommunicated besides."

Linnet held her tongue with the greatest of difficulty, outrage mixed with the astonishing realization that Amy really believed all this with single-minded conviction. Was it possible that Papists didn't see themselves as traitors and assassins, but as loyal and honest people following a righteous course? And, moreover, would they think of her and Colley as being the wicked traitors, spying on friends in their own homes with the purpose of betraying their confidence?

It was a terribly upsetting notion, and very muddling, besides. It made the counterplot seem not much nicer or better than the Papist plot, and her own role distasteful. Did one, then, have to do wrong to prevent another wrong? What would Giles think about it? Would he play the spy, even against traitors? Even to save the Queen?

Her conscience, appalled by this dilemma, retreated in confusion to somewhere in the back of her mind, and Linnet went doggedly on with her role of spy on the traitors. But somehow she couldn't think of anything to say. She just stared at Amy, confused and unhappy. For the first time she realized that they were toying, she and Amy and Colley and the plotters, with lives. Not just the Queen's life, but all the others, too: real people, who might well die as a consequence of what she and Amy said to each other. Amy, with that one incredibly stupid slip of the tongue, could well have signed the death warrant for her parents. And Linnet, with sudden revulsion, felt that she couldn't be a party to it.

The silence had gone on for what seemed a very long time, and Amy was looking scared. "Don't tell," she pleaded.

"I won't," said Linnet impulsively, and felt a sense of relief. In any case, it didn't matter, for Amy had said no more than Colley knew already: that there was a plot afoot to put Mary Stuart on the throne of England. No need for Linnet to tell that. And if Amy, later on, should let slip something else, more important. . . . Well. . . .

"What's the matter?" asked Amy, instantly relieved of her own worry, and puzzled at Linnet's expression.

"I feel confused," Linnet announced with her incurable candor.

Fortunately, Amy didn't inquire further. "That's because you're not converted yet," she asserted, becoming patronizing again, and instantly losing Linnet's sympathy. "Once you are, everything will be perfectly simple and clear, and you'll never be muddled any more."

"Truly?" Linnet challenged. "Do you swear that you never feel confused about what's right and wrong? And things never get all muddled up so that whatever you do is partly wrong?"

"Never," said Amy positively, possibly feeling that a lie was justified if it helped convert a lost soul.

The lost soul at once stopped thinking of Amy as a fellow human, confused and groping even as she, and hardened her heart. Anyone as smug as Amy probably deserved anything that happened.

Conversation languished and died, and both girls were relieved when Mistress Throckmorton sent for them to come to the drawing room.

For once Linnet had no trouble keeping her tongue from wagging. She didn't want to talk; she wanted to think. She sat quietly while the adults chatted lightly of things that didn't matter: that there seemed very little sweating sickness so far this summer, and a new playhouse was to be built in Southwark, and it was said that Queen Bess was still keeping the little French Duc d'Anjou wondering whether or not she would marry him. They mentioned their famous relative Sir Nicholas Throckmorton, who was Ambassador to France and a trusted advisor to the Queen—a bit of information that brought Linnet out of her reverie and into a state of even greater confusion.

And while she was trying to decide whether it was at all wise of Queen Bess to trust any relation at all of the Throckmortons, Mistress Throckmorton excused herself and took Linnet into a small chamber alone, to ask whether she truly wished to become a Roman Catholic.

Linnet cast down her eyes and pleated her kirtle and said she didn't know. After which she raised eyes that were genuinely and disarmingly troubled.

"There, there, poppet, of course you don't," said her hostess soothingly. "How could you, until you've had some instruction? Don't worry, dear; your father has arranged that you shall come regularly to visit Amy and have a little instruction from Father Rodriguez, and you shall think about it after that." And, smiling and kindly, she led the way back to the drawing room, the company, and refreshments.

Linnet continued so silent that on the way home Colley glanced at her curiously. "How now, Sparrow, did the comfits stick your teeth together? You did well, and made a most excellent impression; does that please you?"

"Well, I'm not sure," confessed Linnet. "I mean, yes, of course—but—but I'm not sure I much like doing this, after all."

"What?" He stopped there in the street, tilted up her face, and stared at it in the torchlight while Gregory obligingly paused and held the torch still. "What mean you, Sparrow? Are you trying to tip the double on me at this stage? Because—"

"Well, I'm not," said Linnet staunchly. "All I said was that I don't like having to have counterplots this way even if it is in a good cause, so I'm glad Amy didn't tell me anything you don't know already."

Colley stared for a moment, looking surprised, baffled, angry. "What is't I know already?" he asked at last, very quiet and somehow very dangerous. "What haven't you told me, Sparrow?"

Linnet refused to quail. "Well, I'm not going to tell you, because it was just something you already know, so I promised Amy not to tell anyone. I won't promise that any more, of course, in case she tells me something you don't know, but I did promise this time."

He stared a moment longer, wavering between fury and amusement. Then he broke into laughter that made a passer-by glance nervously over one shoulder and scuttle around a corner. "My dear scrupulous Sparrow, do you really consider yourself bound by a promise made to traitors?"

"Yes, I do," she asserted, scowling.

"But why?" He was deeply curious. "Bodkins, girl, they lie through their teeth to you when it suits their purposes. Just like me," he finished with a laugh. His voice was wondering, condescending, and Linnet resented it.

"That's your affair," she snapped. "And theirs. I dare say you have your own rules, whatever they are. And I have mine. And 'tis not your integrity gets hurt if I give my word and then break it."

"Welladay," said Colley at last in a voice that was subtly changed. Almost, it was respectful. "Do it your own way, then, Sparrow. I care not what rules you follow so long as you do what I want in the long run. But make no more promises of that sort, for I want to know everything that is said to you."

And they turned through the high gate of Over House.

10

Temper

Linnet sat in the small, pretty chamber that she considered hers at Over House, waiting to be called down to supper and trying to pretend that she didn't miss Giles and her family and the countryside. Here she was in the throng and excitement of London, which was what she had always wanted, so why did the luminous greens of Wiltshire in June keep rising before her, glowing behind her eyes, almost bringing the scent of lily-of-the-valley and early roses with it?

At that moment Kitty rushed in, without so much as a knock at the chamber door. "On your shambles, dell," she cried briskly. "Colley says to get you back in your old clothes and take you back to Nether 'Ouse—I mean House—right away. And when—"

Linnet shot to a standing position. "Go back! There?" Her voice rose to a squawk. "Well, I'm not going, that's all! I won't! He said—I mean, he let me think—"

"Ar, and now 'e says to go back." Kitty produced the ragged old kirtle and bodice Linnet had been wearing when she came up from Nether House. "Shake your fambles, wench. You don't argue with Colley; you obey 'im."

88

This was an idea wholly unacceptable to Linnet, who obeyed only her parents, and that grudgingly. "No!" she repeated, stamping her foot. "You can't make me!"

"Gregory can," Kitty retorted laconically.

This was all too true, and Linnet gave in, fuming and furious. Deprived of her pretty clothes and hating the shabby ones, she presently went with Kitty and Gregory, out the servants' door and around and around London. Not, she noticed, the same way Colley had brought her, but on another maze that repeated itself more than once. If she hadn't been so angry she might have tried to figure it out, but she was seething much too much. And once back at Nether House, she expressed her feelings by calling them all brutish miscreants and scum.

The scum, quite a tolerant lot on the whole, snickered and made remarks in cant which she didn't understand, but let her more or less alone. After all, she had nothing to do with them, being from that remote and improbable world of the upper classes. Everyone knew gentry weren't quite human, not having the hearts and feelings of real people. Except for Queen Bess, of course, whose mother's grandfather had been a draper, and who bragged of being "mere English" like the rest of her people.

But this gentry mort, with her curled lip and nose in the air: she wasn't Queen Bess. She wasn't of the common people, either; had she been, they'd have put her in her place at once. As it was, they endured her scorn and hoped Colley would see fit to take her away again soon.

On that point, at least, the Flock and Linnet were in complete agreement. Nether House was more unbearable than ever; and to make it even worse, she was catching a rheum which kept her coughing and sneezing and sniffling, with no kercher, apparently, to be had.

By the evening of the second day, she had reduced the patient Nan to cowed silence, and herself to a state of smoldering misery. And when Colley sauntered quietly through the door, she was ready and eager for battle.

He greeted his Flock before he turned to Linnet, who was lowering at him like a brooding thunderstorm. "Lackaday," he observed, studying her with amusement, fists on hips. "The sparrow looks like a lion. What's amiss this time?"

"You are!" stormed Linnet. "You're a villainous carbuncle! You lied to me, and stole me, and hit me on the head—"

Colley looked greatly diverted. "No, I didn't," he interrupted. "I was across the room at the time. It was Gregory."

Goaded, Linnet jumped to her feet. "How dare you send me back to this verminous place?" she demanded, coming to the heart of the matter.

He looked at her as if she were indeed a snarling sparrow, interesting but not at all important. "It happened to suit my convenience."

"To suit—" she sputtered.

"My dear Sparrow." Indulgence was gone, and his voice was a drench of cold water. "You and your wishes are not of the slightest importance. I shall keep you where I please, when I please; and if I choose that Nether House must put up with you, why then they'll do so. Is that quite understood?"

He received an unexpected answer. Enraged beyond endurance, Linnet doubled up her fist and struck him in the eye with it.

For an instant Nether House was stunned. None of the Flock could quite believe what had happened. A bishop might be attacked, or an ambassador, or even a king. But not Colley, who was only slightly less sacred, perfect, and godlike than Queen Bess herself. Diggory and Joan half rose, dying to strangle Linnet personally. The smaller urchins clutched one another, aghast; Peace yelled, and Alfie blinked in pathetic bewilderment before deciding not to believe his eyes. Only Maudlin went on stirring the unsavory mess in the pot, unconcerned.

Colley recoiled briefly, as astonished as anyone. Then he seized both her wrists in one hand and held her easily, surveying her with interest as she struggled.

"Oh, lackaday," he said regretfully. "I see I shall have to lesson thee, Sparrow." And he held in his other hand the lithe willow switch reserved for such occasions.

It descended. Linnet let out a small choked yelp and whirled in his grasp to stare with incredulous eyes, as much shocked as hurt. The Flock jeered and giggled, and Linnet felt herself go hot and pink with humiliation. She couldn't bear it! Not in front of all Nether House!

Colley's hand raised again, and suddenly Nan was clinging to it, whimpering. "Please," she whined, "don't 'urt 'er, Colley! 'Er's too fine, like. 'Er didn't mean it; please don't! Yer kin beat me instead; is that orl raht?"

Colley paused. He looked derisively at Nan, and then at Linnet. "Well, what say you?" he challenged her. "Shall Nan take the rest of it for you? She's only a brutish tatter-

demalion with no brains or birth or feelings, so it doesn't
matter if—"

How easy it would be. . . . Linnet shook her head violently, and then lowered it so that a curtain of copper hair
hid her face. "Plague take you," she mumbled through it,
and set her teeth.

"Welladay," said Colley again, noncommittally, and
pushing Nan out of the way, continued the punishment.
The audience was perhaps a trifle less derisive now, but
Linnet didn't notice. Still hidden behind her hair, she was
concentrating on not being a baby in front of Nether
House.

"Now up to bed with you, Sparrow," said Colley when
it was over. "I'll make something of you yet."

Tight-lipped, blinking against the tears that welled dan-
gerously along her eyelids, Linnet fled with very little dignity up the sagging stairs, and presently lay curled up on
the pallet she shared with Nan. And then at last she began
to cry, shaking and shuddering with sobs until, after a long
long time, she fell asleep.

She awoke stiff and smarting, and with a sense of having
been used as a shuttlecock or perhaps a tennis ball. She
winced slightly and then peered up through the dimness of
the room at the gaunt devoted face of Nan hovering over
her.

Linnet frowned, first from habit, and then as a certain
memory focused itself, in perplexity.

"Does it 'urt very much?" begged Nan. "It'll feel better
soon, 'strewf; it allus does."

Her concern was deep and genuine, and it caused Linnet

to feel very peculiar indeed. She regarded Nan with a mixture of shame and doubt. "Whatever did you do that for?" she mumbled defensively.

This was greeted with blank silence. "Wot?" asked Nan at last, with admirable brevity.

"Last night," explained Linnet, not very lucidly. "When you—when I've been so shrewish—and you keep acting as if you like me!" she finished, almost reproachful.

"I does." Nan was surprised that there should be any question about it.

Linnet lifted her head so suddenly that Nan jumped. "Well, but why?" she demanded.

Nan was quite unequal to this. "I just does," she said, helpless.

"But—" Linnet found that her lip was quivering, and she controlled it sternly. "I don't deserve it," she said with a humility that surprised herself and alarmed Nan. Had the punishment addled Lady Sparrow's wits?

" 'Ow now," she said soothingly, and dared to pat the nearest arm. "A'course yer does. You'm better nor me," she explained kindly, in case Linnet had temporarily forgotten this basic fact of life.

But Linnet frowned. A number of basic facts in her life had been under considerable stress lately, and why not this? "Why?" she asked, experimentally.

Nan decided she'd best be humored. "Same way I'm better nor a dog." Linnet failed to look completely satisfied at this, so Nan obligingly expounded. "Yer got birth 'n breeding; yer's pretty 'n clever: yer kin even read, haply. You'm gentry."

This was true and unarguable. But—but where was

the virtue in it? Linnet frowned harder, groping with a brand new idea.

"Well, but what did I ever do to merit all that?" she asked.

Nan looked baffled, and with good reason. How could anyone be said to merit what they were born with? Linnet, her teeth now firmly into the matter, worried it. "If Queen Bess saw you in Chepeside, when you were just standing there and not even begging, and gave you a whole basket of oranges, would that make you better than Joan?"

Nan giggled at the absurdity of the idea. "Nar, just luckier."

"Well, then!" Linnet wasn't quite sure what, if anything, this proved, but she felt strongly that whatever it was, it might be important. It had something to do with whether it was really quite fair to judge people by the fortunes of birth. . . . She fell into deep thought.

When at last she ventured downstairs again, toward evening, it was with a somewhat new outlook on the Flock. Alfie was the first to notice it. He was still guarding the door (since no one had told him to stop) when she appeared in front of him and began studying his face as if she had never seen it before. Alfie stared back apprehensively. But she astonished him with a gracious smile, which caused him to gape at her dumbly, like a dog who has unexpectedly been patted instead of kicked.

Linnet almost choked. No one ought to look like a dog grateful not to be kicked. Not even a dog. It made her feel vaguely guilty. But the mute devotion with which he followed her into the common room gave her a warm glow

that increased with every passing minute. Alfie liked her
—as easily as that! She felt oddly rich, and greedy for
more. As the others came in from the day's work, Linnet
found herself looking on them not merely as unfortunates
or lower orders, but as people. Even—even as possible
friends? It was true that exterior appearances were not
very enticing, and it was perhaps doubtful that she would
ever have a great deal in common with any of them—
but then, neither did she with Amy Throckmorton.

When Colley came in that night, it was to a changed atmosphere, much less charged with hostility, somehow.
Was his Sparrow tamed, then? A look at her discouraged
this notion at once, for her shoulders were defiant and her
eyes belligerent as she met his questioning gaze. Colley
chuckled, pleased. Good spirit there, not easily crushed.
She'd shape up well with a bit more training.

"You'll begin your instruction at the Throckmortons'
next week," he informed her casually, and waited for her
reaction.

But if he expected her to beg to return to Over House at
once, he was disappointed. "And what am I supposed to do
in the meantime?" she demanded. "Just go on sitting here
with Nan and Alfie wasting their time guarding me, when
you might just as well let me go out and see London some
more? You know perfectly well I shan't try to run away,
at least until we know more about how to save the Queen,
so—"

"D'you want to beg, then?" he teased.

"No, I don't, and I don't think you'd let me if I did, because you said yourself I look silly dressed as a beggar. I
just want to see London some more. And besides, I get ex-

ceedingly bad-tempered and stupid just stuck here all day, which I should think would be very bad for my instruction. It might make me miss something important I ought to notice, or perhaps say the wrong thing myself, and we wouldn't want that, would we?"

"I think I had best begin training you as a blackmailer," said Colley admiringly. "You begin to show the most remarkable natural aptitude!"

Linnet shrugged off the implied compliment. "Yes, but may I go out and see London?"

"Oh, very well," agreed Colley, and turned to the nightly practice with purses and pockets.

11

Chepeside

Morning found Nether House—indeed, all of Slops Alley—vibrating to the sound of roars. Slops Alley didn't mind, not being fastidious about such things. But Linnet rushed down the rickety stairs to see what on earth was wrong with Peace this early in the day.

Peace stood in a dirty little scrap of shift in the small chamber next to the wardrobe room, bellowing. Beside her was a jug of not very clean water; and a brassy-haired older girl named Peg, with the nominal assistance of Nan, was making feeble dabbing motions with a cloth toward the small bit of face surrounding the wide-open mouth.

"What's ado?" demanded Linnet in a screech to be heard over Peace, who at once stopped her din in order to listen to the conversation.

Peg forgot that she disliked Milady Sparrow. " 'Er first day at 'prentice nipper," she explained, looking harassed. "Colley, 'e said ter make 'er clean 'n respectable, but 'er's bawlin' the place down."

Linnet looked speculatively at Peace, who was clearly gathering her forces to continue. For some reason, she was making no attempt to fight. The skinny arms were limp at her sides, and she stood still, the picture of submissiveness except for her howls. That wasn't like Peace; not if she really meant it.

"Well, she's just expressing her opinion," Linnet guessed shrewdly. "A matter of principle, you know. If she really minded, you'd never get near her."

Much struck by this, Peg eyed Peace doubtfully and made another dab at the small face, which at once turned again into an open mouth.

"Cock's bones, you'll never get anywhere that way!" exclaimed Linnet, seized with an impulse. "Here, let me."

In a moment Peace's yells took on a note of genuine outrage, and she began flailing her arms and legs. Peg and Nan, inspired by Linnet's businesslike approach, grabbed and held the little girl, and at last there emerged from under the scouring rag a fair skin, glowing bright pink with scrubbing and fury.

Peg and Nan regarded it doubtfully. It looked very much out of place, somehow. "I don't think Colley meant that clean," Peg suggested. "Don't look right."

"He said respectable, didn't he?" Linnet argued briskly. "Well, she certainly is. And," she added with relish, "if you're going out with her, you'll have to get just as clean as she is, won't you?" And she set about her own washing, hastily, before the water got any dirtier than it was already.

Peg gave her a baleful glance, not at all sure that this unexpected new side of Milady Sparrow wasn't going to turn out even more uncomfortable than the old. Linnet didn't notice.

"Now if her hair were washed. . . ." she mused, fixing

an enthusiastic eye on Peace's dirty straw-colored mop. Peace made sounds of profound alarm, and hid behind Peg, who glowered. "But of course you needn't think I'll do it for her," Linnet added with a cunning that surprised herself. "Not for anything, I wouldn't. All the same, look how pretty she is with her face clean, Nan. Can you imagine how she'd look with pretty gold curls instead of all that filthy tangle? But 'tis none of my affair, so let us go get dressed. I want to spend all day seeing London." And she led the wondering Nan back upstairs, leaving a baffled Peg and a thoughtful Peace behind her.

It was a golden but sharp-winded June day, of the sort that should never be spent in a hot and dirty city, but in the green-and-birdsong of the country. Surrey, for choice, thought Giles regretfully, taking up his position at the front door of St. Paul's with a kind of hopeless doggedness. It seemed as if he had been searching London for months and months. Was he addle-pated? Was she even now safely at home, where she'd said she was going? It was idiotic to spend the lovely summer here for no other reason than that something quite irrational in his spirit told him that Linnet was here and needed him. Hugh had stopped arguing the point with him, and merely looked pained. Hugh's father clearly thought Giles was losing his wits. And Giles was no longer so certain that he wasn't.

And yet here he was, at his fruitless vigil, because he knew she was in London and could think of no better place to watch for her. He slumped his shoulders against the doorway, discouraged. People swarmed in and out, no

one paying any attention to him. It had been established by
now that he was a permanent fixture—he or one of his
servants—doubtless eccentrics of some sort. . . . He'd
never find her! It was hopeless, ridiculous! If only he'd
hear from her parents! Why hadn't they answered Lord
Crowdon's letter asking whether Linnet had come home?
Perhaps he should write again? It was easy enough for
something to happen to a letter going a long distance like
that. . . .

His mind went on and on, while his eyes stared at the
entrance, so tired after all these days that they sometimes
unfocused, or refused to register what they saw, or even
saw people who weren't there. This was alarming, for suppose Linnet walked right past and his eyes failed to register
the fact?

There, they were playing tricks again, so that the
shabby maid coming in with another girl and a great hulking lad seemed exactly like Linnet. Giles blinked and shook
his head. It still seemed like Linnet! The shabby hood hid
the hair, but— Giles left his doorway and began to follow.

It was Linnet! There was simply no mistaking the ca-
dences of her voice or the way she walked, and presently
she pushed her hood off, so that he could see the apricot
hair, as well. But what in Tophet was she doing in those
clothes and with such unprepossessing companions? In the
act of marching up to her in order to ask these questions,
Giles had a second thought, and paused. Something was
decidedly odd. Why *was* she dressed like a servant? And
why did the two with her hover so closely? He frowned,

considering these things and also the pricks his intuition was giving him. Usually perfectly trustworthy on anything to do with Linnet, it was now strongly suggesting caution. So with a prudence that went very much against his grain, Giles settled himself down to following.

It was very puzzling indeed. Sometimes they seemed like sightseers, and sometimes Linnet seemed to be taking instruction from her odd companions; and the people they seemed to recognize were a very peculiar assortment indeed, none of whom looked any better than they should be, no matter how respectably clad.

Out of St. Paul's they went at last, and up around through Paternoster Row to Chepeside, where they plunged into crowds as into water. This was the widest street in London, and filled with humanity. Here the tall, narrow, timber-framed houses on either side were richly carved and gilded, and some even had glass windows in the ground-floor shop fronts. Stalls stretched along both sides and down the center, and nearly half the crowd seemed to be bellowing "What d'ye lack? What d'ye lack?" in stentorian voices.

Unnoticed in the throng and noise, Giles moved closer to his quarry. He had no intention of losing sight of Linnet now! His eyes remained glued to her back and the sharp little profile that showed every few seconds as she tried (and quite successfully, too) to look at everything at once. Because Giles was watching her so intently, he found himself noticing what she noticed—and an extraordinary series of things it was, too. A small child whipping up a scrap of skirt with professional skill to show the ugly open sores on her leg. A dogfight. A plump blond lady in a litter with servants running ahead to clear the way, who took a sharp second glance at Linnet's coppery hair but failed to see the face which Linnet turned swiftly away. A sober young merchant's clerk, who seemed to cause gusts of mirth from Linnet and her companions, and who gave them an oddly playful threatening gesture. The stalls down the middle selling hawkbells, copper preserving pans, larded guinea fowls, roses in pots. . . . A sandy-haired urchin with rabbit teeth and a snub nose who gave Linnet a cheeky smile and then neatly picked a pocket and vanished.

A great tucket of trumpets and considerable shouting from ahead suggested to Giles that someone important was coming. Someone important but unpopular, he decided, as the tucketing was followed by renewed shouting of a decidedly unflattering nature.

"Way for the Spanish Ambassador!"

London obeyed, but with great reluctance, and only because of the very large armed guard and because Queen Bess didn't like them to be too rude to foreigners. They weren't, felt the Londoners, being too rude: just reasonably outspoken.

"Plotter!" they bawled. "Papist! Assassin! Spaniards, go home!" And then, just to make sure the point got across (Spaniards being notoriously stupid about speaking English) they threw some mud and filth from the most convenient gutters.

Giles grinned, in perfect agreement with London. Don Bernardino de Mendoza was at best an arrogant man who told highly-colored tales to his master the King of Spain and who tried to bully Queen Elizabeth, and at worst was up to his neck in plots to murder her. Giles and London firmly suspected the worst.

They were just warming up, too. More mud was being gathered as the ornate coach approached. With one eye fixed firmly on Linnet (who was energetically shouting insults along with everyone else), Giles was preparing to watch the show when a small pandemonium erupted a few feet away, turned into a snarl of children, and then ejected a small black kitten followed by a straw-haired moppet with an unnaturally clean face. They launched themselves one after the other almost under the front hoofs of the first horse and vanished into the throng on the other side.

The horse reared. The crowd cheered and urged it to trample the Spanish Ambassador. A series of small boys catapulted after the girl, this time just behind the first horse and under the nose of the second. More rearing and cheering, and a great pepper of hot Spanish remarks from the Ambassador's coachmen and guard.

And then, taking Giles completely by surprise, Linnet hurled herself across the path of the third horse, followed instantly by her two companions and a large bosomy girl with brassy hair and a birthmark on her cheek. After which the gaps closed firmly, Ambassador Mendoza's procession passed with all the heavy stolidity of Spanish ships or Spanish farthingales, and most of London pressed forward to tell him what would happen to him if anyone whatsoever should harm a hair of their Queen's head. Giles, using language that would have stood his mother's hair on end, was forced to stand helplessly where he was until the whole thing was over; and then, of course, Linnet had completely vanished.

"Marry!" said an old woman with great admiration. " 'Tis a most wondrous fine bit o' swearin', that, m'lad. But," she added regretfully, " 'e's out o' 'earin' now, that Mendoza is. Best save it for next time. Or the Frenchies." She went off shaking her wispy gray head and muttering darkly about the French. And Giles stood still, sick with disappointment and anger.

Linnet hadn't the faintest notion that Giles had been just behind her for more than an hour, but she had, unaccountably, been thinking of him all afternoon. How very nice it would be to see his blue eyes and stuck-out ears and even his disapproving expression. Moreover, Giles wouldn't fool about and delay over this plot against Her Majesty; he'd do something, and at once. Linnet was sure of that. Suppose the Throckmortons and their plotting friends went ahead and did whatever they were planning while Colley was still wasting time? The fear haunted Linnet, creeping through the back of her mind to thin her new appreciation of the Flock and of London.

Still, it was a glorious day. Alfie and Nan pointed out things she might have missed, though there weren't many. There was Salamon picking a pocket—and Diggory posing as a merchant's clerk and glaring at her whispered jibe—and Peace cutting her first purse. And then came the Spanish Ambassador. He was just the man to whom Linnet wished to speak her mind—and she was now possessed of a brand new vocabulary that would have caused

Giles to clap a shocked hand over her mouth and store several of the most pungent phrases away for his own use in other company.

But she never finished saying what she thought of Señor Mendoza. The snarl of children that erupted was almost at her elbow, and it involved Peace. Trying, as usual, to rescue a kitten. And pursued by several of the meanest little boys Linnet had ever seen. They'd have no mercy on a kitten, nor on Peace, either. Without debating the matter for an instant, Linnet dashed to the rescue.

The crowd on the other side of the horses swore horribly at having still another swathe cut through just as it was getting warmed up. Linnet didn't notice. She ducked and wriggled and kicked and bored her way through, following the sounds of battle. Just between Friday Street and Bread Street, near the entrance to the Mermaid Tavern, there was a deep doorway, almost an alley. Peace stood there, backed against a wall, clutching the squalling kitten heroically against her thin chest, yelling at full volume, and doing battle with the remaining hand and one foot against the swarm of savage little street urchins.

Linnet waded in joyously. In seconds she was planted firmly in front of Peace, and two of the brats were bawling from being seized by the hair and having their heads bumped together with a violence that would have cracked skulls less hard. The others, enraged, began a concerted attack. It was now no longer the gang game of tormenting something small and helpless; it was battle to the death. A dirk was out, and another.

And then Alfie was there; and the gang, whimpering, was being bounced off walls and flung out into the crowd or onto the cobbles like rag dolls. A nice, gentle, compassionate girl would have felt sorry for the poor little brats, who after all were behaving in the only way they had ever known; but Linnet's new sense of humanity didn't as yet go that far. She stood for a moment thoroughly enjoying justice being done. Then a duet of yowls from behind her caused her to turn her attention to Peace and the kitten, who were both exceedingly unhappy. Tears poured down Peace's newly-dirty face as the terrified animal clawed her.

"Leggo!" came Nan's shocked voice, followed by Peg's more commanding one. "Put it down, Peace!"

Peace shook her head. Her small mouth, turned downward in pain, was clamped valiantly shut, and she sidled back along the wall to escape Peg's grasp. She plainly meant to fight off the entire world to keep her treasure, even if the treasure clawed her to death while she did it.

But she didn't need to, after all. Linnet had her cloak off, and swooped it neatly around the screeching fury before anyone could blink. "There," she said, lifting it from Peace's torn arms, rolling it up once more, and then handing it back. "Now let's go back to Nether House and wash your wounds."

They all stared: Peace with incredulous joy, the others with dismay. "You can't take it 'ome!" they told her, shocked.

"Yes, we can," Linnet retorted. "You don't think we'd let it go after all this trouble rescuing it, do you? Besides, Nether House needs someone to catch mice; they're like to drive us out some day and take the place over. Come along, then, Peace; do you want me to carry it for a bit, or will you?"

Peace stared at her for a long moment, her sharp little face looking more peaky than ever with the birth pangs of a brand new emotion. Then, for the first time in her short life, she deliberately gave her full trust to another human being. She put the squalling, lurching, clawing cloak into Linnet's arms and fell into step beside her.

12

Persephone

Separate, either Linnet or Peace was a force to reckon with. United, they were overwhelming. They marched back to Nether House trailing a feebly protesting Peg and a Nan and Alfie no longer protesting at all. There, ignoring Maudlin's scowls, they unrolled the cloak and released a scrawny black whirlwind. It leaped straight into the air with a shriek that made Peace look envious, and then circumnavigated the room twice, screeching disapproval.

"Coo!" breathed Nan, awed. " 'S like a bleedin' bird!"

"Or a mole," added Linnet, as the kitten dropped to the floor, burrowed under the stinking rushes, and began to explore, still wailing, but rather half-heartedly. It had even more curiosity, as it happened, than most cats, and also the soul of a collector. The black triangle of its head popped suddenly up from the deep rushes near Peace, and stared around apprehensively.

"Wah?" it inquired with a rakish air that was largely due to having snow-white whiskers on one side only.

"It looks like Persephone coming up out of the Underworld," giggled Linnet.

"Purse-Effony," echoed Peace, breathing hard and never

taking her eyes off her hard-won pet. " 'At's a good name. 'Er's 'ungry, Sparrow."

"Aye, to be sure," agreed Linnet. "Give her something from the pot, Maudlin, do."

Maudlin grunted in an extremely negative way, and the others looked scandalized. Give food to an animal? Unthinkable! Even Peace looked doubtful.

Linnet was beginning to understand things better than she had. "Call it part of my supper, and I'll take less," she urged, though with a slight pang, for she was hungry enough to eat Nether House fare with relish. "Just this once. Soon she'll be catching mice for herself," she added cunningly. Maudlin might—as they all did—accept rats and mice as an inescapable fact of life, but she still yelped when one ran over her pallet at night.

Peg, who felt the same way, at once took on the air of someone about to be converted against her will. Maudlin looked slightly less negative. They didn't like the idea on general principles; and what Colley would say, they couldn't imagine. Or, rather, they could. . . . But somehow a small pannikin of porridge was grudgingly ladled out and handed to Linnet, who passed it to Peace, who set it down at the spot where the kitten had last emerged from the rushes.

"Purse-Effony," she called in such a soft, sweet voice that they all stared at her, amazed.

The black head reappeared presently, looking astonished. No one had ever offered Persephone food before. Ears flattened, she cautiously approached the dish, wary of the small dirty hand so near. Hunger won.

The kitten was just finishing when the front door groaned, footsteps clattered along the narrow corridor, and Joan and Polly appeared, already fishing loot from assorted hiding places in their clothing. They paused in the doorway to the common room, puzzled by an unusual atmosphere.

"Eee," said the kitten amiably, polishing up the last drop and cocking a wary ear at the newcomers.

"What," demanded Joan, "is that?"

"Purse-Effony," Peace informed her with an air of greatly superior intellect.

"She's going to catch mice for us," Linnet added diplomatically.

A mouse appeared from somewhere under the rushes and cruised past about two feet from Persephone's nose. She stared at it absent-mindedly, her stomach full and her attention on other things. This was a surprising place, but perhaps not so bad, after all. Worth exploring, at any rate. She set off to do so. The mouse prudently vanished. Joan jeered and the others laughed.

"Well, she'll catch mice just as soon as she settles in a bit," Linnet amended, slightly chagrined. The kitten was out of the door now, considering which of the narrow corridors to take, when the door moaned again and a covey of small boys led by Salamon charged in and nearly fell over the small creature, who at once turned into a spitting demon and vanished down the nearest branch of the maze.

"Coo!" exclaimed Salamon, coming into the common room. "Wot was 'at? Devil's cat? I fink I saw 'orns on 'im."

Alfie, who had been silently struggling with a dim and buried idea for at least an hour now, finally remembered what it was. "Ar," he said. " 'At's it. Black cats is witches' cats."

"Who says so?" Linnet demanded at once, aggressively. "How do you know? Can you prove it?"

Alfie, who couldn't in the least remember who said so, and had never heard of proving things, subsided in confusion. He perceived dimly that he had said the wrong thing, and that Sparrow, Nan, and Peace were all frowning at him. They ranged themselves in a solid block against the rest of Nether House, who were uncertain whether to be hostile or amused. Maudlin went on stirring the pot, the door kept up a steady complaint, and the Flock trickled in, heard the story, and took sides. Alfie sidled sheepishly over to stand behind Linnet. And the kitten trotted back, surveyed the crowd doubtfully, and submerged under the rushes once more, either for safety or (as Linnet claimed) to hunt for treasure.

"Besides," she declared, struck by sudden inspiration, "this isn't just an ordinary black cat; 'tis a *black cat with white whiskers on one side!*" Her voice was reverent, triumphant. She paused, clearly giving them time to rejoice. They eyed her uncertainly, never having heard anything special about a black cat with white whiskers on one side, but hating to admit it.

"Didn't you know?" cried Linnet, amazing herself with her own quick-wittedness. "Why, 'tis the best possible luck! 'Tis the mark of—of—Demeter! And it brings wondrous good fortune if you care for it and it likes you, but the most wondrous ill luck if you harm it or cast it out." And she looked menacingly first at Salamon and the little boys, and then at Joan.

Joan looked skeptical. But Polly's eyes widened in her dirty face, and she nudged Joan with a scaly elbow. "Coo, Joan! 'Strewf! Show 'em wot yer got terday!"

Joan blinked, and then slowly drew out of her bodice a fine jewel, worth a small fortune. It was a fabulous bit of loot, and almost guaranteed Joan's promotion soon to Over House. It also turned the tide in favor of Persephone. Especially when Peace remembered the purse she had cut —her very first—and it proved to have gold pieces in it.

This was indeed evidence! Linnet even found herself rejoicing with the others before she remembered that all this stealing was very wicked, and she probably should be warning them about hell-fire. But she found she couldn't. For one thing, it was much nicer not to be a shrew and a spoil-joy. Anyway, if they didn't steal or at least beg, how would they live? As long as Linnet couldn't answer this, she felt she had better not raise the matter.

"Wooh!" said Persephone from under the rushes, and she popped up triumphantly bearing in her teeth an old moldy pantofle nearly as big as she was. A ring of suddenly indulgent and favorable eyes fixed upon her in a manner that might have disconcerted a kitten with less *savoir faire*. As it was, she looked around with an air suitable to Queen Bess, and then trotted back down her chosen corridor to establish a private museum with the pantofle as its first treasure.

Linnet giggled. The Flock regarded her as disapprovingly as if she had laughed at the Queen.

When Colley did his appearing act much later that evening, he found himself standing in the doorway quite unnoticed, staring at a most extraordinary scene. The entire Flock was sprawled amid the rushes on the floor concentrating on what seemed to be a small but active earthquake down below.

After a moment the earthquake appeared, in the form of a scrawny black kitten with an ancient bit of pig's knuckle in her mouth and a defiant air that dared anyone to take it away from her. She headed purposefully for the door, paused for a suspicious slinking detour around Colley's feet (which seemed to make her nervous), and vanished into the corridor.

Colley turned his head to stare after her, bemused. The Flock, perceiving him for the first time, was smitten into uneasy silence. "What," demanded Colley, just as Joan had done, "is that?" And his eye fell quite naturally on Peace as the probable instigator, though what had got into Joan and Diggory and Maudlin he couldn't imagine.

Peace stuck her chin out. "Purse-Effony!" she shouted defiantly. " 'Er's mine! 'N Linnet's, too," she added generously.

Colley turned his surprised gaze to Linnet. The change he had noticed last night seemed to be expanding. Was the little baggage actually encouraging Peace in defiance of his authority? Colley bent an eye of tolerant godly wrath upon them both. "What did I tell you about picking up stray animals?" he demanded of Peace quellingly.

"This 'n's different," she assured him, singularly un-
quelled. It's a lucky cat. 'S got white whiskers on one side,
'n that's lucky."

"Indeed?" An arched eyebrow arched higher. "And
who told you that tale?"

"Ar, but 'tis true, Colley! 'Strewf! Look 'ere!" They all
crowded forward eagerly with their bits of proof, Joan's
splendid jewel in the place of honor. Indeed, it had been an
unusually good day. Colley hesitated. It wouldn't at all do
to have his authority undermined . . . but on the other
hand, it might really be a good luck cat. One heard of such
things. And it might be well enough to have a mouser, in
any case, provided his Flock wanted it, which they seemed
to. . . . Colley liked them to be happy. Contented people
worked much more enthusiastically and efficiently, for one
thing.

Persephone hurried back, having hidden her treasure to
her satisfaction, and sniffed worriedly at Colley's feet. One
could tell a lot by the smell of feet. These rather puzzled
her. She licked one experimentally, and then sprawled ap-
pealingly on her back, both to disarm hostility and for a
better look up at the owner.

Colley raised his other eyebrow, stared down his nose
for an instant, and then laughed and rolled the kitten over
gently with his rosetted leather toe. "I'sooth, I'd like to
train you," he observed. "What a cunning dell you'd
make, to be sure, little wheedler! Welladay." He looked
at them all, especially Peace and Linnet. "Let it stay, then,
as long as your behavior pleases me. You're a clever little
nipper, Peace my poppet; 'twas a nice purse indeed. Now
show me again on the practice one. No need to get cocky;

remember that lad who turned up his toes on the nubbing cheat only last week because he got careless, and he no older than seven. Come along Salamon, and you others." And the nightly practice was on.

But Linnet confronted him later, before he could do his usual vanishing act, fists on hips. "What day next week do I start my instruction?" she demanded. "Oughtn't we to hurry. I mean, the Queen—"

"You don't trust the Queen to take proper care of her own safety, do you, Sparrow?" he observed, amused.

"Well, no, I don't. Because she's much too tender-hearted about that villainous Mary of Scotland, you know. If you were Queen Bess, you wouldn't go on paying a lot of money to keep Mary quite comfortably locked up while she went on and on making silly wicked plots with foreigners to kill you and steal your country, now would you? You'd have had her head off years and years ago, and so would anyone else."

"I warrant!" agreed Colley, much struck by this. "What, then? Are you suggesting that I rush off to Sheffield and execute Mary myself?"

"Well, it would make things a great deal simpler," Linnet began with enthusiasm. "But I suppose you'd never do it unless someone paid you a great deal, and I haven't any money at all."

"Bloodthirsty brat! Aren't you ashamed, Sparrow?" Linnet shook her bright head stubbornly. After all, Mary had started it, hadn't she? "And you scold my Flock for a little thing like stealing!" he went on.

Linnet scowled. "Well, that's different," she protested. "Anyway, you didn't answer me. Shouldn't we hurry? I mean, those vile plotters might go ahead and kill her any minute. Queen Bess, that is. And if we told Walsingham right away—"

"Don't get in a tweak, Sparrow!" He pinched her cheek jovially. "No need to worry. These plots drag on and on for months and years. Every idea they hatch has to be sent back and forth between Mary and France and Spain and London and wherever else the plotters happen to be. You needn't worry. D'you think I'd risk letting a good bit of business slip through my fingers?"

Linnet slanted her right eyebrow scornfully, but there was no use reproaching him, for he had no sense of shame. He nodded affably.

"I'll send for you when I want you. In the meantime I may not be back for a few days, but you may go out again as long as you behave yourself. But—" He smiled suddenly. "No more animals!"

There was a relieved silence when he had gone. Then Peace turned her back on the hawkbelled purses and marched over to Linnet.

"Wot was the other Purse-Effony, and wot was 'er doing under the ground?"

Linnet blinked twice and then grasped the connection. "Oh," she said. "Persephone came back up from the Underworld after Hades stole her, you know."

But of course Peace didn't know. No one in all Nether House had ever heard of a Greek myth—or even of a Greek. Curious eyes turned from pocket practice or kitten-watching, sensing something interesting.

" 'Oo stole 'oo?" It was Diggory, who was the cleverest of the older boys.

"Wot's 'ades?" asked Nan.

"Tell us a story," commanded Peace, coming to the heart of the matter with a bellow that attracted the attention of everyone not already listening.

Linnet was silent for a moment, absorbing this fresh discovery of how deprived their lives were. No myths. No stories, or history, or geography, or languages. No books, of course: books being rare and expensive even with the printing press having been invented over a hundred years ago. Linnet had never before fully appreciated the privilege of being able to read and write. And these. . . . Really, life did seem to be most outrageously unfair, and it seemed up to her to correct the situation as much as she could. And why not?

"A long long time ago—" she began.

"Before I was born?"

"Oh, *much* before."

"Before the Queen was born?"

"Before the Queen's great-great-great-great-great-great-great-great-grandfather was born," said Linnet impressively.

This created an awed and disbelieving silence. Joan tossed her dark head and talked loudly to Polly and Peg, refusing to listen at all. But the others moved closer. Sparrow might be telling wild lies, but this was a talent rather than a drawback at Nether House.

"Anyway," she went on, "there were some people called Greeks, and they were very clever, and built most wondrous buildings and statues, and wrote plays, and everyone went to see them in big theatres. And they had lots of stories called myths, mostly about a lot of gods who lived on a mountain called Olympus, except for Hades, who was god of the Underworld. And one day when he was out riding, he saw this girl named Persephone. . . ."

She had her audience. They listened in breathless silence as she told about the kidnapping and return of Persephone, and then of Theseus and the Minotaur. Quite suddenly she realized that the entire evening had fled and that her voice was hoarse. She stopped. There was a silence, a deep general sigh.

"Garn!" sighed Peg, who had long ago stopped pretending not to listen. "I ain't never 'eard anyfing like that in all me life. 'Ow'd yer ever 'ear such tales?"

"My mother and father told me first, and then I read them," said Linnet apologetically.

"Tell us more!" demanded Peace, twitching at Linnet's kirtle.

"I will," Linnet promised. "I—I could teach you to read," she suggested diffidently.

There was a perfectly stunned silence while they coped with this idea. Diggory gaped, Joan tossed an angry head, and several other heads shook in alarm at the very thought. Reading was not for the likes of them! But Peace and Salamon volunteered at once. Nan followed suit, breathless at her own daring and not sure what it was all about, but willing to agree to anything Linnet suggested. Then Peg, and several of the smaller urchins, joined in. Presently Linnet had a small class earnestly learning their letters, bursting now and again into shrill astonishment at discovering that each of those odd-shaped marks stood for a sound.

"I always thought 'twere magic," confessed Diggory gravely, his deep-set eyes wondering. "This way it don't need ter be magic; it makes sense. . . . Is that the water-coming-out-of-a-bottle-sound one?"

"No, that's the all-out-of-breath one," said Linnet patiently. "You can't learn it all at once, you know, and it must be terribly late. Just remember these three. This is B-b-b for water-out-of-a-bottle; and this is H-h-h, for all-out-of-breath; and here's W-w-w, the wind letter. Now do let's go to bed, or you'll all be horribly clumsy and stupid tomorrow and get caught and end up on the—the nubbing cheat."

They looked at her with approval. Milady Sparrow was turning out to be quite human, after all.

13

The Search

This time it was Hugh who spotted Linnet in Chepeside. It was true that he had never seen her, but after all, there couldn't be very many young girls with apricot-colored hair and a right eyebrow that aimed itself at the top of St. Paul's, and who were accompanied by a large, vacant-faced young man and a gaunt, tall, anxious-looking maid.

With a sigh, Hugh abandoned the hawkbells he was bargaining over, and followed. All the way down to Billingsgate on the Thames, he trailed them, not realizing his luck that it was only Alfie and Nan with Linnet. Any other of Colley's Flock would have noticed Hugh almost at once, and arranged for a highly unpleasant accident. As it was, Hugh thought himself very hard done by, for it was the better part of three hours before his quarry made their way back to Nether House, opened the complaining door, and vanished behind it.

Hugh stood there for a moment, puzzling. The idea of going in after them seemed highly impractical, and in more ways than one. Nor did he like the idea of staying there very long. It was not a very nice alley. It stank more than most, and some very unprepossessing people seemed to be wandering past. Some of them even went in that same complaining door, including the girl with brassy hair and a birthmark whom Giles had described, and some others who made Hugh's hair stand on end. Hastily he made a mental note of the place and swung off around the corner. Much better to tell Giles and let him decide what to do. It would be something energetic, of course. And probably messy. And Hugh himself would be involved, of course, whether he liked it or not. Already was, if it came to that.

He turned a second corner and found himself unexpectedly among nice old houses with walled gardens, and trees showing above the walls. Not the first thing, but good enough for wealthy merchants and lesser gentry. What an extraordinary place London was, where fine houses stood practically back-to-back with squalor! He went on his way quite unaware that there was anything significant in the passing thought—or in the tall man with a pointed beard and fine velvet cloak who sauntered out of one of those houses escorted by a massive bodyguard.

But when he brought Giles back to show him where Linnet had gone, he couldn't find the place at all. He wasn't even sure of the alley. " 'Twas near here somewhere—I think," he mourned, scowling at a row of houses that all seemed the exact duplicate of the one sought.

"Flea-brained idiot!" said Giles, considerably annoyed. "Couldn't you have noticed where it was?"

"I did. Or at least I tried to." Hugh sounded irritated, but it was mostly at himself. He was now beginning to take Giles seriously, and to consider the plight of a delicate (if ninny-noddled) maiden in this sort of place. "Vile neighborhood," he remarked, horrified by what he saw around him, and thankful for the armed servants he had brought with him this time. "All these foul alleys look just alike! I remember that there were quite nice houses just behind. . . ."

His voice trailed away, discouraged. Giles was staring around with an angry, appalled face. He was suddenly furious that people should live like this. Anyone, of course, could have told him that it was perfectly normal and therefore right: the nature of things. Now, faced with it, Giles began to entertain serious and indignant doubts. In the first place, who said it was the nature of things? And in the second place, if it really was, then, decided Giles with the simplicity of greatness, the nature of things should be changed.

He pulled himself out of the rage with an effort, though it had never showed on his mild-looking face beyond a certain flicker of his eyes. Linnet first.

Setting his lips rather tightly, and deliberately shutting out the wretched conditions around him, Giles went on doggedly searching—actually passing Nether House once. But by then Hugh was quite incapable of remembering it. All the houses and alleys had run together hopelessly in his mind. They went home at length in a state of profound depression.

"But my dear boy!" Lord Crowden looked harassed. "What do you expect me to do? I can't search the whole rabbit warren of London!"

"No." Giles conceded this with what he considered great generosity. "But you can lend me some men-at-arms, or even ordinary servants, and let me scatter them around to watch for her. I'll just tell them to follow any young girl with apricot-colored hair and a right eyebrow that points at the top of St. Paul's," he added, forestalling the obvious objection.

Lord Crowden looked relieved to be getting off so easily. "Eh? Oh, yes, yes, by all means. Take a dozen." Giles looked unsatisfied. "Take a score for need. And good luck." And he hurried out of the room with the air of a man who has a great deal on his mind.

Giles looked after him speculatively, and then at Hugh, who had been showing some of the same disquieting symptoms of late. Like people trying to pretend they weren't sitting on thorns. For the easy-going Hugh, this was particularly remarkable, and it suddenly occurred to Giles that it wasn't due to worry about Linnet. They didn't even know her. There was something else bothering them.

"What's amiss?" he asked. "Or is it a family matter?"

"Family matter?" Hugh looked startled.

"Well, you and your father both seem distraught of late . . . and if there should be something I could do to help. . . . If it didn't mean stopping my search for Linnet, of course. . . ."

"I don't know what's amiss with Father," said Hugh flatly. "Mine is a sort of—well, an ethical problem." He looked embarrassed. "The thing is, I don't even know if I've the right to talk about it."

"Well, don't, if you doubt," said Giles at once.

"I think I need to," Hugh decided. I suppose it's my duty to take it to Father, but I can't; he's got problems of his own. In theory, Giles, if you've got one loyalty to your country and Queen, and another to your religion and family . . . what do you do, pray tell?"

"Oh, is that it?" said Giles with considerable sympathy. He had often wondered how Hugh and other Roman Catholics coped with the situation the Pope had put them in when he proclaimed his Papal Bull of Excommunication against Queen Elizabeth. It declared that she was not the true monarch of England, and that they were not her subjects and must render no obedience. In short, it forced English Catholics to choose between loyalty to Church or to country—and added the most persuasive threat of hell-fire and damnation should they decide wrongly.

Hugh was looking at Giles, startled. "You mean you know?"

"I'm not a greengoose," said Giles rather snappishly, and stared at the fine old tapestry on the wall rather than at Hugh's face. "I know you're a Roman Catholic, don't I? But cock's bones, Hugh; I don't know what you should do! You mean you haven't made up your mind?"

Hugh hunched his shoulders and turned to stare out of the window, down to the charming formal gardens below and the Thames beyond, where ferrymen and barges and small sailing boats plied their busy ways. "It isn't that, quite," he mumbled. "Father and I are both loyal to the Queen, mark you, Giles. I thought you meant—" He paused, took a deep breath. "Marry, I don't blame those who obey the Papal Bull; hell's a plaguey uncomfortable place. Only . . . Giles, I think there's another plot afoot. Against the Queen's life. A big one, I mean; more than just the usual sort of thing that goes on all the time. And some of our friends and cousins are in on it."

Giles whistled soundlessly, and his fists clenched with the sharp desire to use them on anyone who threatened the Queen.

"I could be wrong," Hugh went on. "But that little pea-goose Amy Throckmorton keeps hinting about something she calls The Enterprise. I keep thinking it can't really be anything serious if she's in on it . . . but what if it is, Giles?" He turned his pugnacious-looking face to Giles, and on it was a worried look that had never been there before. "Is it my duty to report my own friends and kin, when I'm not even sure about it, and most of England is ready to hang Papists just on suspicion? Can I keep silence and risk the Queen's life? Giles, I'm a traitor either way I look at it!"

Giles stared at him in dismay, all thoughts of Linnet struck from his mind for the moment. "Cock's bones!" he said, and joined Hugh in a long and brooding silence while the clouds scudded across the sky so quickly that the sun seemed to flash in and out like a blinking eye. The tapestry rippled as a brisk breeze blew through the room. At last Giles took a deep breath.

"Faith," he said, coming to grips with the thing in a manner quite beyond Hugh's ability. " 'Tis a case of the lesser evil and the greater loyalty, and that's something you have to decide for yourself. And the only way to do that is to learn more about this Enterprise. No help for it, Hugh; you'll have to flirt with Amy until you can get some more out of her."

"Spying on my friends!" mourned Hugh. " 'Tis a vile thing to have to do! And I don't even like flirting with Amy any more," he added, shoulders sagging. "She's such a complacent, cream-faced little goose!"

"Never mind; think how much worse 'twould be were she the maiden of your dreams," Giles told him briskly. Hugh stared, much struck by this. "Besides, it may be all her imagination, in which case you'll not be spying at all, but perhaps saving her from real trouble. . . ." He stopped, shook his head. "No, no use trying to put a good face on it, Hugh; 'tis a nasty business any way you look at it."

But Hugh was looking much more cheerful. "Certes, you're right, and I shall have to decide one way or another. Can't just sit around and worry until 'tis too late. Besides, I've just had a most brave notion. You can come help me flirt with Amy."

"I've got to look for Linnet!" protested Giles, alarmed. "Besides, I'm not a Papist, so I wouldn't be—"

"So much the better!" Like many lazy people, Hugh could show extraordinary stubbornness when it came to shifting part of the responsibility. "You've no loyalties to betray. You've got to, Giles; didn't I help you look for Linnet?"

"But—" said Giles.

"Oh, yes, Giles Campion. I've heard about you. You're that comical boy staying with Hugh who keeps running around saying his little sweetheart is lost in London."

Giles looked at the speaker with great dislike. Her hair

was a most improbable shade of flaxen, her voice was high
and artificial, and he could not honestly feel that they
would ever become friends. He smiled affably.

"Oh, aye, I'm quite mad," he agreed. "Save only on
Green Wednesdays. Then I become sober, but after one
look at society I do but start foaming at the mouth, and
bite whoever is nearest to hand, and go mad again." He
permitted his eyes to roll just a trifle.

"Oh," said, Flaxen-hair doubtfully, and began hastily to
count up what day it was. She backed away with a nervous
giggle, leaving Giles in possession of the field.

"Rogue!" said another voice, and he looked around to
see his hostess, Mistress Throckmorton, looking both
amused and reproachful. "Did my poor daughter deserve
that?"

"Yes," said Giles firmly, and met her eye. She was a fair,
pleasant-looking lady who didn't at all look like a person
who could be plotting treason and murder.

"Well," she conceded, "mayhap she did. Still, you are
being laughed about, you know." She studied him. "You
don't look mad. What makes you think this girl is in London?"

"I know her," said Giles. "Besides, Hugh and I have
both seen her and lost her again. At least, I think it was
she," he added. "I couldn't mistake that red hair."

"My dear boy, half the females in England are wearing
red hair these days!" An acid note in her voice caused
Giles to look at her with new and sudden interest.

"Don't you like red hair?" he inquired politely.

She laughed, scorning pretense. "What you're really

asking, of course, is don't I like the Queen? You Protestants! You think every Roman Catholic in England is hatching plots."

"Aye," said Giles. "I wonder how we can have got the notion?"

"A touch." She smiled at him as if he were a mature man and not just a boy. "There will always be a few fools, you know. As for the other, of course I wish for a legitimate ruler who would lead England back to the True Religion under the fathership of the Pope. I wouldn't be a good Roman Catholic if I didn't."

"But you'd force all men to be Papist even against their own consciences." Giles frowned.

"Aye, heartily!" She looked surprised. " 'Twould be for your own good, you know, to save your souls."

Giles shrugged. He had heard the same thing often enough, and from both sides, each certain that they had the only truth and the only way to heaven.

"Why not let us all decide for ourselves?" he suggested, knowing that the idea would be shocking and offensive to both sides . . . to everyone, nearly, but Queen Bess, who had once said that they all worshipped the same God and all else was a dispute over trifles. "The Queen allows you Papists to worship as you wish, and even to bring Jesuits over from the Continent to preach and convert. Why will you not be content with that and allow others the same freedom?"

"Poor deluded boy!" Mistress Throckmorton looked sincerely distressed at such heresy. "I would so much like to save your soul." She sighed. "I'm saving a sweet girl named Jennet, and it's such a wonderful feeling. But I doubt you will ever let me. Never mind; let be, and tell me why you think you should be able to recognize this one red head amidst such swarms of them."

"Because no one else has that shade of red," Giles told her, dropping the subject with relief. "It's the color of apricots, and I've never seen such a color on anyone else."

"But I have." She smiled kindly, sorry to be dealing him a blow. "My little convert Jennet has hair just that shade, and I saw it only a few days ago on a little serving maid in Chepeside, as well. 'Tis not so uncommon as all that, dear boy." And she nodded and moved off, leaving Giles in a profound state of discouragement.

14

Lessons

Overnight the new and fascinating game of learning to read had taken over at Nether House. The bell-hung pouches were nearly abandoned, despite Maudlin's sour looks. Everyone was either actively learning letters or taking a deep interest in the lessons—except for Joan and her cronies. And even Joan, for all her scorn, was always there and watching; and Linnet had a shrewd suspicion that she was managing to learn quite as much as the best of the pupils.

The best of the pupils was undeniably Peace, who became unbearably cocky about it until Linnet, with a burst of inspiration, set her to helping some of the slower and younger ones. Then she developed a sweet patience that astounded everyone. (She made up for it, of course, the rest of the time.)

The young ones learned the fastest, on the whole. The older ones (especially Nan and poor Alfie) made heavy going of it, and Linnet began using stories as a bribe. Not until everyone had made enough progress to suit her would she curl up with Persephone purring raucously in her lap and begin a tale of ancient Greece—or of her own home and family and Giles, which to the Flock was just as fabulous and unreal as any myth. They took a particular fancy to the mischievous Hermes—and to Giles!

"Well, they aren't a bit alike!" Linnet informed them rather tartly. "Giles doesn't approve of mischief, and he's always trying to prevent me from having adventures."

"Mayhap 'e just don't want yer ter 'ave all the fun wivout 'im," suggested Peg shrewdly. " 'E usually goes along wiv yer if 'e's around, don't 'e?"

Linnet frowned this off. She had cast Giles in the role of stodgy, muddy-mettled spoil-sport in her modern myths; and although it was not, perhaps, strictly accurate, surely she was allowed a little artistic license.

"He's not a bit like Hermes," she repeated firmly.

"Ar, but us likes 'em both, all the same," said Salamon, giving her a buck-toothed grin and then bending anew over the letters he was tracing on a bare patch of wall. There weren't many bare patches left, most of the lower half being covered with scratched marks. "That time yer fell in the pond together, wot did Giles do to yer arfter 'e pulled yer out? Smack yer?"

Linnet declined to answer this. She was leaning over Nan, who still hadn't grasped the idea that a special shape of squiggle stood for a special sound. What would happen when they got to long vowels, Linnet hated to think. As for Alfie, he had triumphantly learned to make the snake letter—albeit backwards—and was apparently resting on his laurels.

On the other hand, there was Peace. Linnet glanced over at her fiercely defended bit of wall, where the little girl was writing her name.

PEECE, she had written. PEESSE. PEZ. PESE. PEASSE. PEIZ.

PES. PEACE. PECE. PEAS. PEAZE. She looked at them, dirty head tilted to one side. She could not decide which one she preferred.

Nan bent a frowning eye over the N which Linnet had scratched with a bit of white stone on the hearth. "Is it the wind letter?" she guessed hopefully.

"Well. . . . You're closer." Linnet was determined to find some encouraging angle. "But it hasn't got as many lines in it as W, see? Think again. Remember what—"

Something clicked. "Nnnn!" crowed Nan. " 'Tis me name sound!"

Linnet clapped her hands. "Wonderful, Nan! Now can you draw one?"

Reverently if crudely, Nan drew something faintly recognizable as an N. "Nnn," she breathed at it. "Nnn for Nan. 'S another N at the end, too?" she asked, with another flash of brilliance.

This bit of deduction was a remarkable feat for Nan's brain, which was stretching almost out of recognition lately. Linnet was delighted.

"Oh, excellent! Oh, bravely done, Nan! Now mark whilst I put in the middle sound." She did so. "Now there's your name, and you can read it, all by yourself!"

Nan was nearly beside herself with pride, and Linnet with triumph for the both of them. They hugged each other joyfully. Peace, roaring with high spirits, bounced up and down like a ball. Persephone yowled, and all the other pupils stopped what they were doing and made as much noise as they possibly could.

In the middle of it, Colley walked in.

"What's to do?" he demanded into the din, not entirely

pleased at having his entrance go unnoticed—and after four days away, too. They should have crowded around him at once with yelps of joy.

Instead, their minds were distinctly on other things. "Oh, 'ullo, Colley," they said. "Look, Nan's learned ter read 'er name!"

"I kin write mine!" clamored Peace. "I'm best of all!"

"Eh?" said Colley, justifiably confused.

"Sparrow's teachin' us ter read 'n write," they informed him.

"Is she, now?" Colley stood for a moment, studying Linnet and his excited Flock, not sure whether he liked this new development or not. On the one hand, it was to his advantage that they should be even a trifle literate. That sort of thing could be very useful. On the other hand, there were certain subtle changes going on—and not so subtle, too—which needed thinking about. It wouldn't do to let Sparrow instigate too many things. Bad for discipline.

"Welladay," he said, with rather deflating tolerance. "Mind you don't let your new game interfere with pocket practice." And he raised an eyebrow at the neglected pouches over by the wall.

Linnet opened an indignant mouth to point out that learning to read was a great deal better than learning to steal, and he ought to be ashamed of himself. Then she closed it again without saying any of it. What right had she, unless she could provide some other way for them to live? She sighed, and Colley regarded her with amused interest.

"Pocket practice at once," he commanded. "And after

that, Sparrow, I'm taking you back to Over House."

Gloom instantly fell upon Nether House. Who, then, would tell them stories and teach them to read? Peace began to bawl, and the others looked at Colley—for the first time—with something like reproach. He had always been a kind of super-being: half-father, half-god, the only one in the world besides Queen Bess whom they revered and loved. But now that he was taking away something they wanted, he became just a trifle of an ogre. Colley sensed this.

"Oh, fear me not; I'll bring her back to you," he chuck-led. "In the meantime, you can practice with one another, surely?"

They looked doubtful. Besides. . . . " 'Oo's going ter tell us stories?" demanded Salamon, aggrieved. He'd been dying to find out what Giles did after pulling Sparrow out of the pond, and also what happened to those few brave Spartans standing off the whole Persian army at the place with the funny name.

Colley raised an interested eyebrow and glanced at Joan and her friends. "Oh, I warrant Joan can tell you most wondrous stories, can't you, Joan?" he suggested, half mocking.

Joan rose at once to the challenge. "Ar," she agreed, glaring at Linnet. "O' course I kin!"

15

The Enterprise

"There you are, Jennet, pet. Did you have a nice session with Father Rodriguez? Take a comfit from the dish there, and sit down whilst you wait for Amy; the lazy girl is late abed." And Mistress Throckmorton smiled at Linnet with such warmth that Linnet had to harden her heart all over again for the dozenth time.

It was terrible to be a guest and a spy at the same time, even for a good cause! Linnet took a comfit without much enthusiasm, and managed a strained smile as she seated herself on a high-backed chair, reminding herself that however nice the Throckmortons were to their friends (and prospective converts), they were also wicked traitors plotting to kill Queen Bess. Well, they were, weren't they? Papist plotters always did plan to kill the Queen, surely? Besides, Amy had all but said so.

Still, Linnet did wish she had more than Amy's and Colley's word for it. After all, Amy was a flea-brain, and Colley told the truth only when it suited him. . . . She nibbled her comfit with such a depressed air that her hostess took alarm.

"Are you not feeling well, sweet Jennet? There's hardly any plague in London this summer," she added uneasily.

"Oh, I'm not ill," Linnet sighed, with a side glance at Colley, who was looking uneasy. Not for her health, she decided cynically, but lest she might say something that would give the counterplot away. He reminded her of the Spartan boy pretending there wasn't a fox under his cloak taking bites out of him, and she indulged in a small wry grin of satisfaction that for once Colley should be doing the squirming. She prodded him a little.

" 'Tis my thoughts that distract me," she confessed quite truthfully, causing Colley to look as if the fox had begun to chew his liver. But Linnet had known intuitively what she was doing, and Mistress Throckmorton leaped to the obvious conclusion.

" 'Tis the process of conversion," she said. "It often happens so. Satan fights to keep his hold on your mind. Once you drive him out and accept the true teachings. . . ." She gave Linnet the loving look of one who sees a sweet child about to be saved from hell-fire.

Linnet returned it with the scared look of one who feels herself being pushed into it. "Well, I'm not sure I will," she mumbled with sudden obstinacy, and contrived not to see the look of dire warning that Colley shot at her.

But if Mistress Throckmorton needed any final proof that Sir Colin and his daughter were what they seemed to be, this religious doubt provided it. She smiled at Linnet with renewed warmth as a yawning Amy came in, plump and golden in her full lemon overgown and saffron-dyed ruff and flaxen hair.

"You girls run out into the garden, now, and enjoy the sunshine." She beamed at them. "Molly will bring you some refreshments presently, and do be sure to keep your face masks up; 'tis a hot morning and you must not spoil your complexions."

They obeyed, resigned to each other's company, and making the best of it. "Is your hair naturally that color, then?" asked Amy presently as they strolled among the neat geometrical flower beds edged with sky-blue clumps of lobelia.

Linnet put a rather smug hand up to the silken copper mane cascading down her back. "Of course," she said.

" 'Tis a pity," sighed Amy, sympathetic. "I should hate having hair the same color as the Bastard Queen."

For an instant Linnet was completely silenced. Amy took an alarmed look at her scarlet cheeks and outraged eyebrow, mistook the reason, and hastened to say something pacifying. "Never mind, belike you can dye it or wear a wig when you're older. Anyway, haply it won't matter by then, for by next year or perchance the year after, the old harridan will be dead and Queen Mary on the throne."

Linnet's scruples about spying vanished like morning mist, but much faster. She swallowed hard, unclenched her fists with an effort, and managed a smile that caused Amy to back up a step or two and wish she hadn't said anything about red hair. Clearly Jennet was very sensitive about it.

Linnet found her tongue and her wits. "Fustian!" she said scornfully. "That's what everybody is always saying, about Mary Stuart, I mean. People keep trying to get rid of Queen Bess, and their plots always get found out by Walsingham and they end up fleeing the country or being caught and hanged. They seem a great lot of fools to me. I don't believe there's any new plot afoot at all. No one would dare after the last one."

"They would! We do!" cried Amy, stung. "And if you mean Ridolfi, that was years ago, at least ten; and he was a silly Italian whom the Pope should never have trusted. I heard my father say so."

"Well, that's what I mean," Linnet pointed out aggravatingly. "And then there was that idiot ship that set out from Italy to invade us, and got lost somewhere around Africa instead; and then the invasion that landed in Ireland and got wiped out, which was very embarrassing to the Spanish Ambassador, and that was only two years ago. So I think anyone would think twice before trying again, because Walsingham is very clever at learning about things like that." Linnet spoke with urgent sincerity.

"God and His Holiness aren't so easily discouraged, Jennet Collyngewood! 'Tis not Mendoza will be embarrassed this time. If I wanted to, I could tell you things would make your eyes pop out, so there!"

Linnet permitted herself to look extremely skeptical.

"I could!" squeaked Amy, goaded.

"Oh, doubtless," Linnet agreed politely, and yawned.

"You don't believe me!"

"No," agreed Linnet forthrightly. "Well, why should I? Even if there was a new plot afoot, which is easy enough to say, I can't imagine anyone telling you about it. You're only a little girl, for all your talk about young men languishing at your feet, and what's more, your tongue wags."

Amy crimsoned with wounded pride. It made her look

very pretty, but Linnet failed to admire her. "My whole family," said Amy with huffy dignity, "knows about it. Especially my Cousin Francis, who is one of the very chief people in it, and he's always visiting the French Ambassador secretly by night, and the Spanish Ambassador, too. And they smuggle notes back and forth to Queen Mary in the cleverest ways you can imagine, that Walsingham would never guess. And the Pope approves, and the Duc de Guise and his brother are going to invade England at Rye next year—in September, I think—and the Spanish army will invade through Ireland, and all the English Roman Catholics will rise, and the Bastard Queen will be killed before that, so there won't be anyone for the Protestants to fight for even if they want to. And the Holy Father says whoever kills her won't be committing murder at all, but doing God's service. And then Queen Mary will take her rightful throne, and all England will return to the True Faith, and everything will be all right."

It was perfectly patent that Amy was quoting a great deal of this. She couldn't have invented it. Linnet was so frozen by this realization that she sat still on the marble bench for a moment in a state something like shock. Amy, seeing that she had impressed her stubborn guest at last, looked triumphant.

"You must be making it up," Linnet said at last, but without conviction. "Nobody would tell you about a thing like that if it were really true; they just couldn't be so pigeon-brained!"

Amy flushed again, hesitated, and then dashed the lingering doubt.

"They didn't actually tell me," she confessed reluctantly. "But my bedchamber's just over the room next to Father's private study where he talks secretly to Cousin Francis and people. And there's a funny spot in the wall, where if I put my ear, I can hear practically everything." Belatedly, she began to look worried. "I shouldn't have told you, Jennet! 'Tis a most tremendous secret, and Father'd flay me if he knew I even knew at all! Please don't tell him, will you! Not a word!"

"Of course I won't tell your father," said Linnet with perfect truth and not the slightest twinge from her conscience.

Amy looked relieved. It never occurred to her that Linnet hadn't promised not to tell anyone else.

"Are you sure?" demanded Colley, tense and intent. "You're not making it up, are you, Sparrow?"

"Well, of course not!" she said wrathfully. "How could it help the Queen if I did that? Besides, I'm not clever enough to make up anything that complicated; and I'm more clever than Amy, so she couldn't have made it up, either."

Colley looked faintly startled, as he occasionally did when she said something sensible. "Welladay, Sparrow; you're becoming most shrewd." Then he instantly forgot her and fell into a thoughtful silence.

Linnet bore it as long as she could, fidgeting. "Well, hadn't we better hurry and go tell Walsingham and the Queen at once?" she demanded.

He stroked his pointed beard and shook his head, eyeing her sadly. "How you do rush into things, Sparrow! No, no; not yet, my dear."

"Well, why not? We shouldn't wait; they might hurry it up or something. Besides," she added with a flash of the realism she was rapidly developing, "the sooner we tell them, the sooner you'll get the reward money, you know."

"My dear Sparrow, you must not try to run this yourself. You lack both sense and experience, and the female brain can never grasp essentials."

"What about Queen Bess's brain?" muttered Linnet.

Colley ignored the question, merely regarding her with that disarming smile that had never yet failed to reduce her to submissive apology. "Don't you trust me?" he asked with deep reproach.

"No, I don't," she stated.

Once again, gratifyingly, he was looking surprised—and a trifle annoyed—and somewhat approving as well. "That's excellent wise of you, Sparrow. I've told you before, you're entirely too credulous. But this really isn't the time to start being difficult with me, you know. We have" —he looked virtuous—"the Queen to serve."

"Well, that's exactly what I've been saying." Linnet eyed the door through which supper might reasonably be expected to appear presently. They ate well at Over House, a fact which she very much appreciated. " 'Tis you keeps saying no hurry, but there is a hurry, because besides saving the Queen, I've got to get home or at least back to Guildford. Any day now Giles is liable to notice that I haven't written or sent for the rest of my things or anything, and then goodness knows what he'll do."

"Presently, I tell you." He nodded at Kitty, who came to announce supper. "In the meantime, we continue your visits and your instruction from the Jesuit. But first, as soon as we've supped, Gregory will take you back to Nether House for a few days, until your next visit."

He looked at her, waiting for the explosion. It didn't come. She was quite pleased, she found, to be returning to Nether House, despite the dirt and fleas and terrible food. It was much more interesting than either Over House or the Throckmortons. She liked the business of teaching the Flock to read, and telling them stories. It was like feeding the starving, only better, because the mental food they gobbled so hungrily would stay with them always.

She was welcomed back! Her appearance was greeted by the younger ones almost as if she had been Colley himself, with roars of approval, and a clamor for an immediate reading lesson, and a spate of news about how Persephone had actually caught a mouse—quite by accident, it seemed, and to the equal astonishment of captor and captive. Alfie beamed at her, and Nan wept, and Diggory grinned, and even Maudlin actually looked at her and nodded: a rare gesture of good will. Only Joan and her coterie seemed something less than pleased.

Linnet produced a packet of fine white bread and saffron cake and gingerbread that she had shamelessly stolen from Colley's kitchen (with the help of Kitty and the cook), and then scrambled away, laughing, to avoid being trampled by the Flock.

"Sparrow!" bawled Peace, swallowing an enormous morsel of cheese whole lest anyone filch it from her. "Sparrow, c'mere!" She rushed over to the wall, where, dimly visible in the evening sunlight filtering through the window, Linnet perceived the evidence of the Flock's industry. Every inch, up to the highest reach of Diggory and Alfie, was covered with scratched letters and words, and even, where Peace proudly pointed, a whole sentence. Linnet squinted at it. It seemed to be an experiment in spelling.

PRS EFNY CATTE COTTE MWS

CATT ETT BOEN BWN BONNE BONE BOWN BOAN

"Persephone Cat caught Mouse. Cat ate—er—bone," translated Linnet, half by intuition and half by practice. "Oh, that's splendid! Did you do it all yourself, Peace?"

"Ar," said Peace, twisting her feet with pride. "But which bone is the right one?"

Linnet looked them over carefully. "Well, all of them," she explained. "I mean, they all say bone, don't they? There isn't any right and wrong spelling so long as the letters come out to the right sound. Here, see how many ways you can spell—um—bread and cheese."

There was a rush for the wall. Presently, after much labor and muttering and heavy breathing, the glorious phrase was immortalized by almost every possible combination. Including SSSOVVIVS from Alfie, who had now mastered the shapes (if not the sounds) of four whole letters.

"Me, I'm the cleverest of all," bragged Peace with more truth than modesty. "I can talk like a fine lady, too," she added in a quite creditable imitation of Linnet. "If I put on a fine dress everyone will fink—think—I'm a gentry mort."

"No they won't," Linnet told her crushingly.

Peace instantly attacked her with both fists, roaring. "They will! Why won't they?"

Diggory plucked her off, and Nan boxed her ears. Linnet waited for the howls to die down a trifle. "Well, for one thing, ladies don't act like that," she said severely. "And for another, anyone could look at you and tell you come from Slops Alley. Ladies—I mean gentry morts —do wash once in a while. All over, I mean. Not very often, perhaps," she amended fairly, "but sometimes. And I shouldn't think you'd ever be brave enough to do that. Remember all the fuss you made over washing just your face? Now, Nan—" She looked at Nan. She discovered something. There was a small, almost-clean patch in the middle of each cheek. "Nan, you've been washing!" cried Linnet, delighted.

Nan blushed, ducked her head, simpered a little. "Thought I'd give it a try," she confessed. " 'Tain't so bad if yer 'olds yer breath."

Peace, her glory snatched away from her, wrenched herself loose from Diggory's relaxed hold and fled roaring to Joan for comfort. Linnet ignored her. Nan and Salamon and Peg were explaining that they were almost out of wall space, and how about taking up all the rushes and using the floor to write on? Linnet privately thought this was a most excellent idea, whether they wrote on the floor or not, and told them how clever they were to have thought of it. Giles would have been astonished at her developing sense of diplomacy.

"You're supposed to teach us to be like gentry," Peace bellowed from Joan's arms. "Me, especially. Colley said so. 'At's why 'e brung you 'ere, innit?"

Joan laughed nastily. " 'Strewf! Well, partly. 'Er sat there on the road like a blubber'eaded flat, just beggin' ter be scrobbled—so 'e scrobbled 'er. Matter o' principle."

Linnet instantly forgot her diplomacy. "Well, the idea!" she bristled, uncomfortably aware that there was a good deal of truth in the unsavory remark, but not for a moment ready to admit this to Joan. "As a matter of fact, I agreed to come help Colley find out about a new plot against the Queen. You don't suppose I'd have just come along for no reason, do you? I mean, now I've got to know you and got used to the food and all, I'm glad about that, too, but that's not why I came, not in the least. It was for Queen Bess."

She had touched the heart of their loyalty. Love of the Queen came before all else to most Londoners. Queen Elizabeth could have had their lives at a whim, walked across their willing backs to keep her feet dry. She was mother, father, child, and God rolled into one. She was their Gloriana, friend and protector, one of themselves. She ruled by the grace of the people rather than the grace of God, and she never forgot it. She defended their freedoms, she cared for them with all her heart, she stood as a frail but unbreakable bulwark between them and the greedy ambition of France and Spain and the persecutions of Papistry. And with all that, she was tolerant. Far too tolerant, surely. Live and let live seemed a mad and dangerous notion; dangerous to Queen Bess herself above all. Ministers and advisors, Parliament and people scolded and nagged her for her leniency—and loved her the more.

The Flock was at once with Linnet. Even Joan thawed grudgingly. After all, since the Queen wouldn't protect herself, it was their duty to do it for her, and this took precedence over everything, even private quarrels.

"That Mary Stuart ort ter watch 'er step," Diggory pointed out darkly. "Anyfing 'appens to Queen Bess. . . ." There was no need for him to finish. Everyone knew. Mary's fate at the hands of the enraged English would be sure and unpleasant.

"If I were Queen Mary," said Linnet thoughtfully, "I'd be working my head off to keep Queen Bess safe instead of the other way around. I think Mary must be as silly as she is wicked."

"Ar," agreed Joan with a sigh. It was a great concession, agreeing with Sparrow about anything—but there it was. The Queen came first, and anyone serving Her Grace simply had to be tolerated, however objectionable.

16

Because of a Bath

Previous morning sounds in Nether House were nothing compared to the ones which awoke Linnet the next day. She rolled off her pallet and rushed down the stairs to the wardrobe floor below, neck and neck with Joan and Nan. The noise came, as before, from the washing room, used only by Linnet herself now and then, or (begrudgingly) when a particular role and Colley demanded it of one of the others. And even Linnet found herself making the effort less often, now she was no longer trying to maintain the greatest possible difference between herself and the Flock. It was a terrible chore carrying pails of water all the way from the conduit in Faiture Lane and up the rickety stairs.

But someone else had apparently been doing just that. Through a barrage of noise they could see that the water had been squandered in a shocking way, pools of it on the floor, a bucket overturned, and in the center of it all, a small drenched scrap of child surrounding an open mouth.

"Peace!" Joan shouted above the din, smacking the scarlet cheek in order to get attention. "Wot d'you fink you're doin'?"

"Being a gentry mort!" yelled Peace, squeezing out a

whole stream of tears that blended at once with the other water on her. "Don't like it! 'S cold 'n wet!"

Joan glared at Linnet ferociously. "You 'n your gentry talk!" She looked at the shivering child, lifted a strand of the soaked mat of hair, and shrugged despairingly. "Wot we goin' ter do wiv 'er now?"

Linnet snatched the nearest garment from the floor and wrapped it around Peace. "Well, I think we should give her a good washing in hot water, now she's already wet. Do you think Maudlin would let us use the other pot? Stop crying, Peace; you won't have any more cold water. It'll be nice and warm, poppet; and you'll like it, I promise."

Joan, on the verge of boxing Linnet's ears, suddenly stopped and eyed her thoughtfully. A narrow shaft of sunlight had somehow penetrated through the narrow window from between the tall roofs around, touching the shining copper of Linnet's hair and the dull yellow-gray of Peace's. Beneath the hair, the two faces were remarkably similar. Sharp and pointy, with the same kind of bone structure. Supposing Peace were scrubbed clean. . . .

Abruptly Joan changed her mind. "Ar," she nodded. "Finish up, now 'er's started. I'll stay 'ome 'n 'elp. Nan, you c'n go out wiv Polly. Alfie c'n go fetch more water. C'mon, you," she added commandingly to Linnet, and led the way downstairs to cope with Maudlin about the matter of heating the water.

It was a spectacular morning. Peace had completely changed her mind about the desirability of cleanliness, and fought like several tiger cubs whenever Joan brought the sodden cloth anywhere near her. Her skinny, naked little body flailed wildly. Then Linnet had an inspiration. With a sudden grab and heave, she lifted Peace and deposited her bodily in the huge pot of warm water. A tidal wave arose to slosh over Linnet and Joan and engulf the interestedly watching Persephone, who fled screeching.

Peace gave one deafening bellow, and then stopped. An expression of beatific joy spread over her face. She blinked, smiled, and settled into the soothing warmth around her until her sharp little chin was nearly submerged. "Coo!" she crooned. "This is naffy, Joan; I likes it!"

Linnet and Joan looked at each other. Almost, for an instant, there was laughter and rapport between them. Then they turned to the new problem: not how to get Peace near the water, but how to get parts of her out of it long enough to scrub. And the matter of the hair was a major battle that required reinforcement in the shape of a sour and disapproving Maudlin.

When they had finished, nearly everyone was as wet as Peace, and the floor had become a kind of marsh, with scummy pools spreading among the rushes. Persephone sat on shore complaining about the flooding of her hunting grounds. Peace sat in Joan's arms blinking sleepily while Linnet dried the clean pink flesh and tangles of soft fair hair.

"Aren't you the pretty poppet!" Linnet crooned. "I knew you would be!"

Peace looked smug, and Joan astonishingly maternal. Like children playing dolls, the older girls bustled upstairs and dressed Peace in clothing suited to her new state of cleanliness, while Alfie labored below to dump the rest of the water into the street.

"Now we'd best start untangling her hair," decided Linnet, producing a battered comb Salamon had stolen for her. "I can hardly wait to see it all combed and tidy. 'Twill be lovely, all silky and golden and curly."

" 'Strewf!" agreed Joan with an enthusiasm that was almost instantly dimmed. In a few moments the air was thick with shrieks and curses and Maudlin had to be called in again; Persephone had fled once more, and the would-be combers were looking at each other with despair. It was doubtful if Peace's hair had ever been combed in her life, and it was even more doubtful that it ever could be.

"Forget it," advised Maudlin with practical cynicism. But the dark head and the copper one shook in unison. In a way, Peace's hair looked almost worse clean and matted than it had dirty and matted. Something would have to be done.

Joan stuck the comb with difficulty through the least dense bit of the rat's nest, achieving nothing at all but a new medley of yowls.

" 'Ave ter cut it," she decided sadly.

Peace stopped her imitation of a major battle and looked interested. "Ar," she agreed with enthusiasm. " 'N tell Colley an 'air-nipper got me."

Linnet and Joan looked at each other.

"He deceives us whenever he feels like it," mused Linnet as if to herself.

"Females is more'n a match for men any day," Joan reflected with conviction. "Even Colley," she added with far less conviction. Clearly she was wavering. Linnet applied encouragement.

"We could say Peace ran and found you after it was cut

off, and we washed it and bathed her to make her feel better," she urged.

Joan looked tempted. "Polly 'n Nan'll keep mum . . . and Maudlin?" Maudlin looked noncommittal, meaning she was washing her hands of the whole affair. Joan nodded and then frowned as she thought of something. "Wot about Alfie? 'E knows, and 'e's a blubber'eaded tongue-flapper."

"Cap downright as Colley'll cock up Sparrow's shambles if any cove squeaks beef on 'er," Peace suggested shrewdly.

To Joan's evident surprise, Linnet gurgled irrepressibly. "You've got a noddle on your squeeze, Peace," she retorted in kind. "But if you go around looking like a gentry mort, you really ought to see if you can say that in gentry talk."

Peace didn't turn a hair. "Vow to Alfie that Colley'll kill Sparrow if anyone tells on her," she said in perfectly respectable accents, and then lapsed at once into broad Cockney. "'Ow's that? Din' fink I c'd do it, did yer? Naffy, innit?"

Both girls giggled, and Joan went to fetch a knife. When the operation was over, Peace wore a short cap of pale gold. They surveyed her with tremendous satisfaction.

"No one 'd think 'er could be a nipper," decided Joan gleefully. "Not even if 'er got caught. . . ." She broke off reflectively, thought it over for a moment, and then bawled for Alfie. "Bring some more water," she commanded briskly. "I'm gorn to 'ave a baff, meself."

They went out nipping and foisting that afternoon, resplendent and shining. Linnet accompanied them, wearing an aura of disapproval which the others treated with the tolerant contempt it deserved. But she went, despite her strong feelings about all this purse-cutting. It was that or stay home with Maudlin.

Still, her conscience, though very much confused of late, compelled her to make a feeble protest. "Ladies—I mean, gentry morts—never cut purses or pick pockets," she told Peace.

" 'Er don't want to be a real lady, blubber'ead," explained Joan impatiently. "Just ter look like one, see?" But Peace looked thoughtful. Perhaps, hoped Linnet, she had begun to get into the spirit of this new role of gentry mort?

Reading and pocket practice were both nearly eclipsed that evening by what threatened to be a plague of baths. The practical uses of cleanliness had suddenly been discovered, not to mention the pleasures, which Peace was shouting about at the top of her voice. Her fair head flitted about the squalid room like a fine wax candle amid the old rushlights, the focus of every eye.

But then Maudlin quenched the bath fever by ruling sourly and with a minimum of words that every bath-taker had to bring in the water, heat it over fuel he had stolen himself, and then empty the water and clean up the mess. "You"—she glared at Joan, Linnet, and Peace—"can do yours now, 'ear?"

Persephone punctuated this pronouncement by picking her way over the marsh with an air of someone in great danger of drowning, implying that she found it most distressing to have to dive for treasure instead of merely digging.

Joan, who didn't often get ordered about even by Maudlin, and did not take kindly to it, looked furious. Linnet scowled, too, and then cheered up suddenly.

"Never mind, we were going to get rid of these vile old rushes, anyway, and use the floor for writing on." Gingerly she picked up a small handful of rushes near the corner where it looked slightly less dirty than the rest, and marched down the corridor toward the door. There was a whoop and a rush, and after that no one seemed to notice that she did no more of the work, but merely stood back and cheered them on. Actually, Joan did notice—but then Joan was doing the same thing, so she could hardly complain. She and Linnet exchanged glances of grudging respect, both hoping devoutly that Linnet would not be staying at Nether House much longer. Two queens in one hive would be one too many.

Persephone, after a few moments of loud dismay, suddenly threw herself into the spirit of the thing, for buried treasure began to emerge in all directions. Mad with excitement, she raced in turn after treasure that scurried away and treasure that lay where it was, taking both to her private collection at the far end of the corridor. The former was more tempting, but it showed an annoying tendency not to stay in the collection. Every now and then Persephone, trotting around a corner with a new item, would meet an old item running out again, and take after it with an indignant yowl. Linnet, laughing so hard there were tears in her eyes, forgot everything else in the antics of Persephone.

Presently it occurred to her that she had never seen Persephone's collection. Taking a rushlight, she followed the kitten down the corridor, past the staircase, and around the switchback at the far end, in the very back of the house, where long poles and boards leaned in a careless pile against the wall. There, just behind the boards, was the hoard. Linnet examined it while Persephone hovered jealously. There were assorted bones, odd rags of clothing, the worn pantofle, some quite recent skeletons of mice, a dead spider or two, several old purses with cut strings (discarded once they were emptied), and— Linnet laughed aloud. Two purses not yet emptied, a hawkbell from the practice pocket, and a gleaming necklace—all prigged from the priggers!

"I won't tell," she assured the worried kitten.

Persephone jumped suddenly into the lap of the squatting Linnet. Linnet at once fell over sideways, nearly dropping the rushlight. "Wicked thing!" she scolded, giggling again, and then stopped, to stare instead with a puzzled frown at the wall she had just fallen against.

There, in the corner under the tops of the leaning poles, was a distinct crack in the wall. Only not an old wall-crack, but a straight, purposeful strip, half an inch wide, like the edge of a door. In fact, it *was* the edge of a door. Linnet proved this very simply by pushing at it. It obligingly opened further, with a silent ease suggesting that it was used rather frequently.

Used by Colley! Linnet had no doubt of this. It explained why his comings and goings were so seldom announced by the grating and bang of the front door, or even a flash of sulphurous fire. He came through here, and just went on down the corridor to the front door and into the common room from there. And he went back the same way. Back to— A flash of inspiration struck her. Back to Over House, of course! It must be quite close, then . . . and they really had been going in circles every time they took Linnet there or back, for the express purpose of deceiving her! She hadn't been imagining things at all. And she wasn't as stupid as everyone seemed to think, either, for she had now found out the secret that not even the Flock knew. Linnet was intuitively sure of that.

Her taste for adventure rushed back, undimmed. What fun! She must follow the passage at once, and see where it came out, and if Colley was at the end, she'd jump out and say boo, and then inform him loftily that he needn't go to all that trouble trying to deceive her any longer. For the short remainder of her stay in London, she could simply eat and sleep at Over House, and just slip through to Nether House for lessons and company and such things.

Persephone, clearly a kitten of Linnet's own mettle, sniffed excitedly at the open gap.

"Oh, very well, if you insist," agreed Linnet happily, and the two of them were just stepping through to adventure when Peace's bellow cut raucously through the maze of passages.

"Sparrow! C'mere! Shake your shambles! Us 'as put all the rushes out in the street, and now us wants ter learn more readin' 'n 'ear some more about Giles and your family, 'n that 'Ermes cove, 'n the mort wot 'ad snakes on 'er noddle for 'air."

Peace clearly relished this last bit, and just as clearly would not stop until she found Linnet. Linnet considered going on with her exploration and closing the secret door behind her; but then with a prudence most unusual for her, gave up until a better moment should present itself. Tomorrow. She closed the door carefully.

"Coming," she called.

17

Silver Ha'penny

Once again Linnet awakened to the familiar roars of
Peace—with a difference. This time she wanted a bath.
At once.

The rows of pallets along the floor heaved and grumbled
in the thick sultry heat that already oppressed the city in
the early dawn. Joan lifted her dark head and snarled at
the howling child. Maudlin reached out a long arm and
slapped. Nan hovered, bleating anxiously that "warshin's
un'ealfy." And Peace, ignoring them all, went on bellowing.

Linnet raised herself to an elbow and shouted above the
din. "On hot sticky days like this, cold water feels best."

Peace paused and eyed Linnet doubtfully. "But I likes
sittin' in the nice 'ot water," she explained. "Feels good.
Wants ter do it every day."

Trust Peace to go to extremes! "Well, nobody does it
that often," Linnet declared firmly. "Not even the
Queen."

Peace subsided for the moment, baffled. Linnet lay back
on her pallet and remembered that secret door.
Today. . . .

"Yer comin' out terday?" asked Peg, her cheerful grin wrinkling the livid birthmark that covered her cheek.

Linnet shook her head and tried to look wan. "Too hot," she murmured. "I always feel faint in the heat."

And then for the rest of the day she had to endure the constant attention of the too-devoted Nan.

Giles paused in the middle of Chepeside, and felt that he was being smothered in heat and despair. It was all most oppressive. A murky look about the western sky hinted at a storm to come, and Giles fervently wished it would hurry and clear the air. His blue eyes, probably permanently narrowed by now with so much searching, roamed the crowds. His purse was tucked well into the breast of his doublet and his hand rested near it at all times. He had been learning a great deal lately about the habits and habitat of the underworld. He found it all extremely interesting.

Just under his nose a sandy-haired urchin with a snub nose and teeth like a rabbit slipped a skilled hand toward a fat purse on a fat merchant. Giles, who was in a foul humor anyway, felt no particular urge to meddle. The merchant was overdressed and overfed and pompous, and Giles had begun to resent the shocking contrast between rich and poor. He turned a blind eye to the urchin and frowned. He had begun to suspect that Lord Crowden's letter to Linnet's parents had never been written, much less sent. No one believed Linnet was in London: everyone either tried to humor Giles's evident madness, or snickered at it. Only this morning Hugh had said frankly that he was sick of hanging about London looking for some silly wench who wasn't even there, and that he was going to go play tennis instead. Giles had retorted with some spirit, and the two parted rather cross with each other.

And Giles, for his part, was feeling crosser every moment. He ran a finger under his ruff, which was prickly and hot on this muggy day, and a perfectly ridiculous garment anyway, now he came to think about it. Whoever invented— His eye fell once again on that sandy-haired urchin, who was now sidling up to a woman who did not look as if she could afford to lose her purse.

Memory clicked. This was that same young cutpurse who had seemed to know Linnet on that unfortunate day when he had found and lost her! Quick as thought itself, Giles's hand reached out and grabbed the bony young arm before its owner could vanish.

The child jerked, failed to get away, whirled to face him.

"I never done it!" he cried automatically. "Lemme go! I ain't got nuffin' o' yours!" he added in genuine outrage. "I never touched you; I never!"

"I know it," Giles chuckled, hanging on firmly. "Fear me not, young rascal; I only want a few words with you."

"What's to do?" It was the fat merchant, looking as thunderous as the weather. "Have you had your purse stolen, too, boy? Have you caught the thief? Search him!"

The boy's round eyes rolled at Giles in terror, and Giles could see the bulge under his rags that was almost certainly the merchant's purse. It would surely hang the child if found. Giles immediately edged his own body between the bulge and the merchant, but he kept a firm grip on that frightened arm.

"Search him!" insisted the merchant peremptorily. He struck Giles as being an offensively overbearing man. "Here I'll do it."

Giles held strong natural objections to being ordered around; moreover, he felt that his position—not to mention that of the terrified urchin—could easily become awkward. So he took unfair advantage of social distinctions.

"Not at all, my good man," he said in the bored but kindly tones of aristocracy (or at least gentry). "My purse is quite safe, and I merely wish to talk to the child for a personal reason; nothing to do with you."

He nodded haughtily, and the merchant, at once deflated, made off, muttering. Giles turned to his captive, who had stopped struggling and was staring up at him with disbelief.

"Now do you believe I mean you no harm?" asked Giles.

The boy hesitated, his eyes shrewd. Then he half-nodded, indicating a readiness to be further convinced. "I never took nuffin'," he asserted.

"Fustian!" laughed Giles, low-voiced. He poked the bulge. "That isn't belly, my lad. Now come along while I'm in such a generous mood; I want a few words with you." The boy was looking apprehensive again, reminding Giles of a very young donkey about to balk. He hastily applied a carrot. "If you can tell me a few things I want to know, I'll give you a silver ha'penny, and you won't even have to steal it."

This was a different story. A silver halfpenny was not to be sneezed at. The urchin came without more ado, those pale wary eyes beginning to look upon Giles with a cautious approval that Giles at once encouraged by stopping and buying a sweetmeat from a woman in a stall.

"Now," he said presently, the grip on the arm no longer being necessary. "I'm looking for a girl. She's fourteen, and she has hair just the color of those copper preserving pans, and a funny eyebrow." He pointed to another stall just ahead, gleaming with polished copper, and then peered down hopefully at his young companion, who didn't bat an eye.

"That'll be Sparrow," he said with assurance. " 'Er's told us abaht you. You'm Giles, wot saved 'er from the pond. 'Er says as 'ow you doesn't like adventures, but us finks yer really does, 'n you'm just like 'Ermes 'n them Spartan coves. Now wot abaht me silver 'a'penny?"

Giles recovered breath and equilibrium with some difficulty. It was true he had picked this urchin because of seeing him grin in a most familiar manner at Linnet, but this seemed too good to be possible. Yet it was too accurate not to be true . . . except. . . . "Sparrow?" he repeated dubiously.

"Colley calls 'er Sparrow, so us does, too. She's another sort of bird, I fink. Wot abaht me rhino?"

Giles handed over the coin, resisting a strong temptation to hug the grimy child. "There's more if you can tell me more," he said hastily, lest he lose his gold mine.

There was no need to worry. It would have taken a great deal to pry Salamon loose, now.

18

Eavesdropper

It was evening and the Flock beginning to trickle back, wilted in the oppressive heat, before Linnet could shake her solicitous nurse and slip away through the maze to that mysterious door at the end of the corridor. Persephone appeared almost at once, rubbing against her ankles and mewing excitedly.

"Oh, very well, but don't tell," agreed Linnet, pleased to have company in this exciting new adventure. Giles would have been better, of course, but she reminded herself firmly that Giles would probably have muttered darkly about doing such reckless things as this, and then wanted to lead the way.

The door was closed this time, and would not push open. Linnet scowled at it, reflected for a moment, and began to feel around the rough wall. There had to be a catch, that was all. It gave suddenly. She pushed the door half open, peering into the solid black oblong and refusing to think that, after all, it might have been nice to have Giles go first. She put a foot in and groped. Stone stairs, going down steeply. Persephone, doubtless fired by the thought of more buried treasure, pressed softly past her ankles and vanished downward into the dark. Encouraged,

Linnet took another step, and then another. Pleased with her own foresight, she remembered to find the catch on the inside. Then she closed the door and instantly was in thick dark that crowded her eyes and was too much even for Persephone, who came pressing back.

"You wanted to come," said Linnet between her teeth. If she let the kitten out now, she might never get any further, herself. And that was silly, because Colley used it all the time, didn't he? She was certain of that. Encouraged, she felt her way down the dozen steps and then forward along a low, narrow passageway that must be completely underground.

It seemed to go on and on in the pitch dark, but probably it was no more than sixty feet before it turned abruptly to the right and then presently into another flight of steps, this time going up. Linnet discovered this by the simple method of banging her bare toe on the bottom step. For an instant she had to sit clasping it and rocking back and forth with the pain while Persephone stuck an inquiring head under her arm.

In the silence there came the faintest throb of sound from above. Voices. Unastonished, Linnet unclasped her toe and began climbing with infinite care up the stairs, grinning to herself as she pictured Colley's face when she should suddenly appear from his secret passage. She had no doubt at all that this was Over House, that it was Colley up there, probably in his study, talking to a guest. Or that the passage would end presently in a door to that same study.

The voices became louder, until they were just on the other side of the wall that rose before her. Linnet, in the very act of raising her hand to find the catch that must release the door from this side, paused. Her grin faded to a thoughtful look. What if Colley failed to appreciate the joke? The more she thought about it, the more it seemed to her that this was likely. For one thing, he might not care to have his guest know about his secret. Perhaps, after all, it might be best to wait a minute or two, if only to see who was with him, and what his mood might be. . . .

She was at once glad she had waited, for the other voice rose suddenly with a kind of plaintive outrage. It was the tone Linnet's own voice had held when she first realized Colley wasn't an honorable gentleman, after all. She drew a deep breath and listened shamelessly.

"But—but that's— By St. Patrick, you're not threatening to betray us! . . . are you?"

Colley's voice was all wounded virtue. "Certes, no, Francis; how could you think such a thing? I'm but being honest and telling you that I am much torn. My new religion wars with my old loyalties, and my conscience needs encouragement of a kind to help convince it of its new values."

The other voice wavered. Linnet recognized it now: it was that of young Francis Throckmorton, the one who was deepest and most enthusiastically in The Enterprise. She had met him only once and hadn't thought much of him, for he seemed both weak and silly, but now she felt rather sorry for him, for he was being reduced to a state of doubtful apology that was all too familiar. And she could easily sense the panic that must be in his heart as he answered.

"We—we thought you were fully converted! You said you had no doubts! We were sure of you, or we'd never have told you about The Enterprise."

"But you didn't tell me, did you?" Colley was at his most benignly and infuriatingly amused. "I told you, didn't I?"

He was toying with Throckmorton, and his victim knew it. "How did you find out?" he demanded sullenly.

Colley laughed. "Genius. Or magic. Or a traitor among you. The point is, I do know, and I'm willing—nay, anxious—to help you. If you just settle my last lingering doubts. Complete my conversion, as it were. With something concrete and convincing." He paused, seemed to think it over. "Gold would do, I warrant." His voice became mellow and reverent. "Aye, gold is a most wondrous fine persuader, don't you think? There's something so solid and reassuring about it. . . ."

"I'm damned if—"

"My dear Francis, we're all of us damned if Walsingham finds out. Especially you. Chief agent for Mary, aren't you? Pay regular visits to the French Embassy by night, don't you? Oh, just to send harmless greetings to your uncle in France, of course. And is the Spanish Ambassador your uncle, as well?"

There was heavy breathing from the young man. Linnet could imagine his rather pale face going paler still, and had to remind herself that he was a traitor and didn't deserve her pity. Was Colley guessing that Throckmorton was Queen Mary's chief agent, or did he know? Amy had hinted as much, and it must be true, for he hadn't denied it,

but only made those muffled breathing sounds, like someone in pain. Or fear.

"What do you want?" he asked.

"I told you. My poor troubled conscience—"

"A pox on your poor troubled conscience!" muttered
Throckmorton, rallying slightly. "Pardieu, Sir Colin: you
argue circles around me, but I'm not such a fool as that!
We're in this for the True Faith; you care only for profit,
and all you want is to be bribed not to betray us to Walsingham."

"You do put things so baldly," murmured Colley,
clearly unashamed.

"You've no honor or scruples at all!" wailed Throckmorton. "How could we trust you not to turn around and
betray us the minute you had your gold?"

"Francis!" Colley spoke in the hurt tones that used to
reduce Linnet to abject apology. "You wound me! Moreover, you wrong me. D'you suppose I'm not sensible to
that aspect? D'you think I'd ask you to trust me without a
guarantee of my good faith?"

"Oh?" Francis Throckmorton sounded almost as mystified as the silently eavesdropping Linnet felt. Up to now
she had seen what Colley was up to, and was shocked but
not greatly astonished. It was just like him to blackmail the
Papist plotters and then turn around and sell the information to Walsingham, after all. As far as Linnet was con-
cerned, this made him far more wicked than the Papists,
who were risking their lives for something they believed
in, however vile and base it really was. But what was this
about a guarantee? It must be another clever trick—
mustn't it?

Clearly Francis wondered the same thing. "What guarantee?" he asked, sullen and suspicious.

"Don't worry." Colley laughed. "One that will convince even you. I've thought it all out, together with another guarantee that will protect me from any—er—unfortunate accidents."

He sounded terribly sincere. A horrible thought struck Linnet. What if he had decided that, after all, there was more profit in milking the plotters than in Walsingham's reward for information? It seemed all too likely. It would explain why he kept delaying, and why—

"What guarantees?" Throckmorton was asking again.

"Why, I'll tell you," began Colley, but he didn't. For Persephone, indignant at being ignored for so long, or perhaps thinking there might be food beyond that wall, suddenly gave voice.

"*Wooh!*" she yelled.

From the study came instant and ominous silence. Linnet didn't wait to find out whether Colley would investigate the secret door in front of Throckmorton. She felt her way back down the stairs with all the silent speed she could manage, her heart crowding unpleasantly in her chest, and her shoulderblades prickling. Back along the dark passage, groping blindly, until she stubbed her toe again on the other stairs. This time she hardly noticed, but just scrambled up, fumbled the catch, nearly panicked, got the door open, slipped through, closed it behind her, and stood with her back against it for an instant, panting and trying to think.

"*Wooh!*" complained Persephone from inside.

Linnet turned and started to open the door again, and

then stopped. If Colley found the kitten in there, he'd assume he shut her in, himself, on his last trip. But if he didn't find her in there. . . .

Linnet took a deep breath. "I'm sorry, sweeting," she murmured through the door to the wailing kitten. Then she scurried through the maze to the passage leading to the common room, her mind in a whirl. Colley was going to betray the Queen; she was sure of it! What should she do?

"Sparrow!" It was the faithful Nan, self-reproachful at having lost sight of her charge, and alarmed at the apparent result. "Coo, yer looks weevily! 'Tis the 'eat; yer better lob yer groats 'n then—"

"Stubble it," ordered Linnet almost absent-mindedly, and found her eyes fixed on Joan, who had just arrived with Diggory. Joan bent shrewdly observant eyes upon her and demanded to know what she was in a tweak about.

Linnet hardly hesitated. " 'Tis the Queen," she blurted. "She's in terrible danger. I must go see Walsingham myself!"

This was greeted with uneasy silence. Was Sparrow betwaddled? She sounded fit for Bedlam, that terrible madhouse just outside Bishopsgate. And just when they had got to like her, too! Diggory shook his head regretfully and said as much. Polly sighed, Alfie looked blank, Nan sniffled, and Peace prepared to howl, but Joan gave Linnet a long, calculating look.

"Wot d'yer mean?" she asked bluntly.

"Colley's tipped the double," said Linnet, equally blunt. "He's going to play along with the Papists' newest plot. It's a huge one they call The Enterprise."

Derisive hoots greeted this. The Flock stood massed against her, and Linnet felt very small and uncertain, and as alien as she had on her first day here. Then Nan silently moved to stand at her shoulder, and Peace took up a ferocious posture on her other side, and Linnet found new courage.

"Gammon!" said Diggory with scorn. "Colley wouldn't. Wot makes yer fink 'e would?"

"Heard him say so," returned Linnet succinctly.

"When?" demanded Joan, her intelligent eyes speculative.

"Just now."

They looked at her. She hadn't been out that door all day. Nan, who knew this better than anyone except perhaps Alfie, looked as if she had been slapped. Thoughts of Bedlam arose again.

Linnet set her lips defiantly. "I'll show you!" she snapped. And she led the way, with stiff, angry steps, through the maze to that switch-back end and the apparently blank wall. The nearest half-dozen peered over one another's shoulders into the gloom, saw nothing whatever, and regarded Linnet with increasing doubt.

"Wooh!" said the blank wall plaintively. Linnet hesitated, remembering why she had intended to leave Persephone inside. Then she shrugged, stepped forward, and opened the hidden door.

Persephone shot out, furious. Someone had locked her up in the dark, all alone, and now, it seemed, they were going to steal her collection. Leaping to guard it, she turned upon the Flock a prolonged hiss that startled even her, and quite unnerved them all. They were in a mood to be unnerved easily. There loomed that black empty hole in their own house, infinitely menacing. Anything might come out of it. They backed up, and turned daunted eyes to Linnet for an explanation.

She gave it, briefly and in a low voice, every bit as scared of that door as they were, and with better reason. When she had finished, none of them felt the least bit better. It was clear even to Alfie that the something which was most likely to emerge from the door was Colley. They didn't think he would be pleased to find them there.

"Close it," said Joan with a small shudder.

Linnet obeyed, not having the heart even to suggest putting the kitten back inside. Then they scurried back to the common room, feeling chilled despite the sultry heat of the city, and clustered around Linnet, waiting.

" 'Tis how Colley comes and goes without making the front door squeak," she said softly, speaking mostly to Joan now. It all depended on Joan. "It was open a crack when I went to see Persephone's collection, so of course I had to go see where it went."

They stared at her, awed. Clearly they had underestimated the courage of their Sparrow, gentry mort though she was. Then, breathing a little easier out of sight of that door, they went back to the issue at hand. They could see no great problem. The Flock had two deities, the Queen and Colley, and that one should betray the other was literally unthinkable. They refused point-blank to think it.

"Garn," they said in tones of finality. " 'E'll take the Papists' rhino and then tell Walsingham, blubber-noddle."

"Well, do you suppose I didn't think of that?" retorted Linnet. "Even Throckmorton did. And Colley said he had an absolutely positive guarantee for him, and—"

"Ar," said Polly. " 'E would. 'E's clever, Colley is. Don't get your tail in a tweak, Sparrow; 'e wouldn't do nuffin' ter 'urt Queen Bess."

"He would if it paid him enough," Linnet retorted with the bitterness of disillusion. Never again would she believe quite so easily in appearances, in plausible charm. Colley, she decided, must be a great deal like Mary of Scotland. Both had that rare ability to win hearts with frightening ease—and neither, apparently, had any scruples whatever. Colley, in addition, was clever, very clever indeed (which Mary apparently was not). Linnet shivered. "He'd do anything if it paid him enough. He's good to you all because it profits him, but if it would profit him more to have your throats slit, well, he'd do it himself and smile whilst he did it. And you know he would."

They looked uncomfortable. No one denied it. Perhaps they accepted it as being perfectly reasonable, or at least one of the facts of life, like cold and hunger and plague. In any case, they felt, Sparrow was confusing two separate things.

"Ar, but 'e wouldn't do nuffin' to 'arm the *Queen*," Diggory repeated.

"That's right, my goslings." They whirled. Colley stood in the doorway, cocking a merry eyebrow at them all, looking amused and reproachful and benign. "Come, has my Sparrow been telling sad tales about my wickedness?" It was perfectly clear even to the most jaundiced eye that here was a man to be trusted to the death. Even Linnet's extremely jaundiced eye wavered for an instant. Then she remembered her new and hard-won cynicism.

"Yes, I have," she said defiantly.

Colley strolled in, tousled her hair, cast an interested glance at the bare, rushless floor, and perched himself on the edge of the table. "What sort of sad tales?" he asked interestedly.

The Flock answered all at once, in a confused and indignant medley in which there was no word at all of secret doors or passageways. They all knew instinctively that this was better unmentioned.

"Stow your gab," he told them good-naturedly after a moment. "Sparrow, how did you come by such a silly idea?"

"Well, I heard you with my own ears," she blurted. "You told that Francis Thr—" She stopped, with the sickening sensation of having just tramped on thin ice and feeling it break beneath her. Colley, who must have suspected where she had been, now most certainly knew. What a fool she was! She must keep him from finding out that she had told the Flock about that door. . . .

Panicky, she flicked a quick glance at Joan, whose eyes mirrored her own thoughts, and who spoke instantly into the blank silence.

"We let 'er trick us," she confessed to Colley in an aggrieved voice. " 'Er must 'ave snuck out while we was throwing out the rushes. When 'er came back, she said as 'ow she'd been to your 'ouse 'n 'eard you talking wiv the Papist plotters." Her eyes were rueful, puzzled, candid. It was an altogether remarkable performance, staged by a born actress. And Colley, still not suspecting the extent of Linnet's subversive influence, swallowed it. He glanced with brief question at Maudlin, but she merely went on stirring the pot. And he smiled.

"What a havey-cavey Sparrow it is," he said mildly. "Welladay, as you're so set on coming back to Over House, perhaps you'd best come along now. As a matter of fact," he added lightly, "haply I shan't need your help any more, and can send you along home."

Once this would have brought a delighted smile to Linnet's face, and the Flock's as well. Now a cold chill seemed to sweep the stifling room. Not for a moment did Linnet believe he'd let her go now. She remembered what he had said on that first day, about finding her corpse in the Thames. Her bones felt as if they were all running together. And there was nothing at all that she could do—or say. She looked despairingly at Colley's genial face, and then at the Flock, who wore the wooden expressions of people determinedly not knowing something they knew very well.

" 'Strewf," mumbled Polly. " 'S a naffy fing for 'er ter go 'ome, innit?"

Some of the youngest ones, not understanding, began to sniffle. Who, they demanded, was going to teach them reading and tell them stories about Giles and Hermes? They were quelled instantly by a fierce look from Joan.

"Close yer chaffers," she said in a hard voice. "Good riddance." She glared at Linnet, who was too numb with fear to notice or care. Nan, belatedly grasping the situation, suddenly turned pasty pale and clung dumbly to Linnet's arm.

But mute acceptance was not for Peace. She set up a shrill screaming that made all her previous efforts seem negligible, and attacked Colley with fists, feet, and teeth.

"Lackaday," said Colley mildly, and knocked her halfway across the room. "Naughty temper, gosling. Come along, Sparrow; we've a lot to do if we're to visit Walsingham tomorrow."

This remark didn't cause the immediate relief that one might have expected. The gray silence continued. For the first time Colley seemed slightly disconcerted, and his joviality somewhat forced. "Come, come, my dears; you don't really suppose I'd let anything happen to Her Grace, do you? Come, Sparrow." And with a hand like iron around her unresisting wrist, he led her out.

There was total silence in the common room. Every ear followed the footsteps down the corridor to the front door. It groaned open and shut. No one moved. The Flock was better trained in guile than Colley knew. After a moment there came soft footsteps, a faint creak, a whisper of skirts against a wall, a tiny sound of wood on wood, and then more silence. Still no one moved. Then Persephone stalked in to announce indignantly that her collection had been invaded again, and they all breathed.

But not yet easily. Not until Joan had sent some of the smaller children to chase one another on a game of tag through the maze, and they had come back to report it was quite empty.

Then Peace picked herself up from the floor, bruised but not greatly damaged, and fled with a heartbroken yowl to Nan's totally inadequate bosom. They wept together while the others stared with morose eyes at them and at the barren floor, still innocent of rushes and writing alike, and looking somehow reproachful.

"Never finish learnin' ter read now Sparrow's scrobbled," mourned a tow-headed urchin called Jack. Alfie knocked him down.

"Gonner kill meself!" sobbed Nan, surveying the Sparrowless void of the future.

"I'd liefer kill Colley," announced Peace blasphemously, beginning to recover her natural truculence. The others stared, shaken at such sacrilege. "Kill Colley!" she repeated. "Save Sparrow and Queen Bess!" Her voice rose to a roar.

"Stubble it!" ordered Joan so harshly that Peace stopped at once. "And stop napping your bib, Nan." She had stood unmoving all this time, staring at the doorway expressionlessly. Now she looked around at them. "Sparrow twigged true," she said flatly. " 'E might leave the Queen in the nitch . . . if 'e can keep the Papists paying 'im enough."

There was no scoffing this time. If Joan said it, they must take it seriously. They did so, dirty faces screwed up with concentration.

She was right! They looked at her and at one another, shaken. Was their first duty, then, to Colley or the Queen? Their faces went blank with the pain of conflicting loyalties.

But only for a moment. To a Londoner one had to come before all others. They sighed, and Joan took command again. She looked around at them all and faced facts, unflinching.

"No use bleating," she said. "We'll just 'ave to blab."

They breathed deeply and waited for her to go on. To whom must they blab, and how?

"We'll go tell the Queen," Joan decided with the simplicity of genius. If the Queen was in danger, clearly the Queen must be warned.

"Gammon!" snorted Diggory, his deep eyes narrowed. "They'd never let the likes of us near 'er. Any'ow, she's on Progress. Cambridge, I fink, or Lincoln, or summat like that; 'n 'ow'd we get there?"

Joan was daunted, but only for an instant. "Then we'll go tell Walsing'am, like Colley was going ter do." She nodded her dark head, and glared around, looking for any further signs of opposition. But there were none. Even Maudlin sat still, seeming neither to approve nor disapprove. Joan took another deep breath.

"We'll go now," she decided bravely.

There was a screech from Peace and a hoarse bleat from Nan. "Wot abaht Sparrow?"

The Flock looked at them. Sparrow? It was the Queen who mattered. Sparrow was nothing if Her Grace was in danger: Sparrow herself would be the first to say so. Besides, they pointed out sorrowfully, it was now too late to help Sparrow. Colley had scrobbled her. No one could help . . . except, possibly, amended Peg, the Queen herself. In any case, the sooner they set off, the better.

Crowded together, as if for mutual protection, the Flock headed determinedly out of Slops Alley toward Candlewick Street, and Ludgate, and the Strand, and Whitehall, where, presumably, Sir Francis Walsingham might be found.

But not all of the Flock left. Some, like Salamon, had not yet returned from work. Others were too young, or too hungry, or had arrived too recently to know what was happening. And Peace and Nan, with one glance of perfect agreement, had already slipped quietly into the narrow corridor leading to Persephone's collection.

Pale with their own temerity, they regarded the blank wall in the near-dark. It was Peace's clever mind and fingers which found the catch, and Nan who pushed the door open to peer doubtfully into the black tunnel beyond. Trembling, they stepped in. Clutching each other, they groped as Linnet had done down the narrow darkness until they stumbled on the far steps, and mounted to the blank wall at the top.

Once again Peace found the catch, but it was Nan's long, scared face that ventured first through the opening, to peer around the shadowed study. It was empty. The silence pressed around them. Peace entered the study in a small silent rush and ended at the door in the far wall, staring at the latch as if it might peck her. Then they both turned to look at the black oblong gaping behind them in the murky light from the window. For although the sun would not set for a couple hours, it was on the other side of the house, and little enough light at best came down the narrow canyons between jutting upper stories. But even in the dimness that opening was far too obvious. Together, the girls closed it; and then, breathing hard, they returned to the door leading from the study.

They listened intently, and then opened the door a tiny crack. Small sounds came from the front of the house, presumably from Gregory doing some duty or other as footman; and from the top of the house, drifting down the stairs, came a faint murmur of voices. Colley's pupils glanced at each other, squared their thin shoulders, and proceeded to be a credit to his teaching. They moved through the doorway and melted into the shadows of the hall, without a sound.

19

Lion's Den

Giles and Salamon were by now fast friends. Giles knew everything Salamon could tell him about Linnet, Colley, Nether House, the Flock, and the roguery business in general, and Salamon was the richer by several silver pennies. Moreover, there was more to come as soon as he had guided this generous new friend back to Nether House. Life was good.

They walked briskly along Three Needles Street, contentedly munching the bread and brawn which Giles had bought from a hawker, and then turned into a maze of narrow lanes and alleys where Giles lost his bearings almost at once.

The sun was still high, but it cast a faintly lurid light, caused by the thin edge of the clouds that were massing higher and higher into the western sky. They weren't muttering thunderously—yet—but one felt that they would at any moment. Salamon eyed them distrustfully and edged slightly closer to Giles. It made him uneasy. So did a thought that had just struck him. Perhaps Colley might not altogether approve his telling a strange gentry cove— even the mythical Giles—all about them, and bringing him to Nether House without permission. He paused on the cobbled streets, dubious.

"I better take yer ter Colley, first," he decided, poised on one dirty foot.

Giles hesitated. Although he had conceived a strong and altogether irresponsible desire to confront this rogue of a Colley, good sense dictated that he try to get Linnet away with a minimum of fuss and bother. And Colley seemed highly likely to create a fuss and bother one way or another. . . .

" 'Tis Linnet I want to see," he pointed out.

"Ar, but Colley's Upright Man, see? 'E'd 'ave me skin if I done summat 'e didn't like." He looked worried. A cove couldn't do much without his skin. "I'll just take yer ter Over 'Ouse instead o' Nether 'Ouse, 'n you can tell 'im yer wants ter see Sparrow. But yer needn't tell 'im I brung you, or blabbed. Need yer?" His light eyes pleaded.

"Not a word," Giles promised, and meant it. They moved on in a state of mutual satisfaction.

Linnet, towed unresisting behind Colley, thought at first they were going out by the front door, for Colley led her straight there. But then he paused, gave her an expressionless glance, and opened and shut the door. It grated, squealed, squealed again, and banged—leaving them still standing inside.

It was a trap for the Flock, of course. Linnet realized it with a new surge of panic. Briefly and wildly she considered making a noise that would warn them—but that would tell Colley there was something to hide. Besides, she daren't, in the teeth of his white smile.

In any case, it was all right. The Flock weren't trapped so easily. The silence from the common room betrayed nothing. In a moment Colley shrugged, nodded, and began leading her through the maze to his secret door, so quietly that only sharply concentrated ears could have heard them from the common room.

Linnet had stopped worrying about the others, and even about the Queen, who, having practically the whole of England ready to die for her, seemed considerably safer at the moment than she was. She stumbled a little in the darkness of the passage, fighting terror. She wanted her mother and father. She wanted Giles. She wanted to burst into tears and scream and throw herself on the ground. But pride and a new sense of acumen prevented her. She would not abase herself before that vile, condescending rogue! And besides, it would, she felt sure, do far more harm than good. So she set her teeth on her lower lip in the dark, and fought for self-possession.

The door at the other end opened, as she had guessed, in Colley's study. Two wineglasses still stood on the table where a guest had sat quite recently. Colley closed the door, released her wrist, and turned to gaze down at her quizzically.

Linnet faced him, hoping she looked a great deal bolder than she felt. "What—what are you going to do to me?" she demanded huskily.

Colley laughed. "Incorrigible Sparrow! Don't look so frighted, my poppet; I shan't serve you up for supper."

"Well, I never thought you would," she retorted, feeling more herself. "But, I mean, are you going to throw me into the Thames or something like that?"

"Why, not just at the moment," he chuckled, apparently not in the least annoyed. " 'Tis not dark enough yet, for one thing. But I do think we had best keep you out of mischief for a while, Sparrow. You're such a meddlesome little minx, and not nearly as tractable as a female should be." Linnet made a rude noise at him, and he looked amused. "Spirited wench. I may yet train you as my doxy, after all—but you'd have to learn to be as obedient as my kynchin morts, first."

Linnet stuck her lip out, but made no comment. Who was she to undeceive him? Besides, her surge of courage was waning, and fear was creeping back. All he had really said was that he wouldn't throw her in the Thames before dark. She shivered in the sultry evening air.

Kitty appeared, and Colley nodded to her. "We're going to keep Sparrow here for a while," he said blandly. "No, not in her usual chamber, where any prigger might climb in the window, or Sparrow perhaps accidentally fall out of it." He frowned, clearly not happy about keeping her at all. For a moment he looked like Jemmy the gardener contemplating a weed, and Linnet shivered again. "I think the small room at the top of the house will serve for the night," he concluded at last, and led the way out of the study, through the hall, and up the stairs.

Linnet followed passively, with a sense of reprieve that she knew perfectly well was illogical; but she had half expected to be slaughtered on the spot, and it was a tremendous relief to be told she might live until morning— whether it were really true or not. Kitty brought up the rear.

The attic room had only a narrow slit of a window, facing northwest, where the sun burned like molten bronze through thickening clouds. There was a narrow pallet and a three-legged stool, and that was all. Linnet imagined being kept prisoner here for years and years. Then she imagined the more likely alternative, and bit the inside of her lip hard to keep from disgracing herself.

"Very comfortable indeed," said Colley, at his most benign, and then paused as a knock sounded at the front door far below. Might it be Francis Throckmorton with the gold? "I'll be back presently, Sparrow. Be good until then." And with a smile that set her teeth to chattering, he closed the door behind him, and locked it noisily, leaving Linnet alone with her very frightening thoughts.

Salamon delivered Giles to the front door of Over House and then prudently took to his heels. Giles, neither surprised nor dismayed, took a deep breath and knocked.

The door was opened presently by a bulky fellow who reminded Giles irresistibly of a wild wolf doing his best to pass for the family dog. He eyed Giles with suspicion, seemed about to slam the door in his face, and then looked again, taking in the well-fitting sapphire hosen, fine damask doublet slashed with lime satin, snowy linen ruff, and jeweled rapier hanging from a silver belt. Another young cock for Colley's plucking? Gregory hesitated. It seemed quite possible. But on the other hand, no one got into Over House without some sort of credentials.

Giles put on an air of insouience. "I wish to see—er —Master Colley," he announced, the insouience rather spoiled by his not knowing what title to give an Upright Man.

Gregory, perceiving this, began to swing the door. " 'E's out."

"Then I shall come in and await his return."

"Yer won't. Carn't come in 'ere." Gregory stood massively athwart the wide entrance, almost—but not quite —filling it.

"I can, you know." Giles slipped neatly under the uplifted arm, feeling pleased with his own audacity. He felt like St. George ready to demolish any number of dragons, until an infuriated dragonish sound from Gregory behind him caused him to skip nimbly but quite without dignity across the great entrance hall toward the stairway.

A tangle of rushes deliberately wound itself around his feet, and Giles found himself sprawled ignominiously at the foot of the stairs, staring at a pair of fine rosetted pantofles which had just come down them.

"What's to do, Gregory?" demanded a cool voice that stopped the burly doorman just as he was about to fling himself on Giles. It also caused two other hurrying servants to pause where they were, alert and obviously armed. Gregory began to sputter explanations.

Giles, abandoning all pretense at audacity or even dignity, propped a resigned chin on his hand and looked up. Up gorgeous magenta hosen, slashed satin trunks and splendid emerald doublet, past a ruff as wide as a cartwheel to a face like Mephistopheles, with dark pointed beard and deep brown eyes. Giles blinked. Mephistopheles was staring down with mild interest.

"Cock's bones!" said Giles with candid astonishment. "Are you Colley?" He had expected something altogether different.

"To my friends I'm Colley," said Mephistopheles, raising his eyebrows in a way that should have utterly destroyed Giles's savoir faire if he had had any left. As he didn't, it left him unmoved.

"Cock's bones!" he said again, in wonder.

Gregory rumbled again. "Soft, now," said Colley, amused. "I doubt not the—er—young man has what he feels are excellent good reasons to come visiting without his manners." And he smiled again in a way that should have caused Giles to feel like a small boy caught in the comfits by his hostess.

It failed. Giles didn't even notice, in fact. He was busy picking himself up from the rushes and sorting out his thoughts. Missing the sarcasm altogether, he simply answered the question. "Oh, aye," he said. "Excellent good reasons. I've come for Linnet."

Colley should surely have looked guilty, or at least faintly startled. He didn't, of course. "A linnet?" he repeated, mildly inquiring. "Not a city bird, my lad, and this isn't an aviary. You'd best search the countryside, or haply settle for a town bird like a starling or sparrow or—"

"Right," interrupted Giles briskly, catching him on the word. "I'll settle for Sparrow." And this time he had the satisfaction of seeing those brown eyes narrow fractionally. "At once," he added, looking as severe and threatening as his regrettably mild face would permit.

Colley's eyes narrowed still further, and then widened. His face took on an expression of amused disbelief. "You can't be Giles!" he cried.

There was a sudden flurry of movement at the tapestry halfway up the first flight of stairs, and an instant later a gust of hot wind blew sharply in at the casement, causing all the candles to flicker. No one noticed that the tapestry moved before the breeze hit it.

"You can't be Giles!" Colley was repeating in amazed tones.

Giles glowered at him, momentarily disconcerted. "Why can't I?" he demanded.

"Because—" Colley leaned against the wall, twinkling. "Because Giles is a poor-spirited sort of fellow: the soul of prudence: a dash of cold water on anything the least bit exciting or adventurous: a tame sort of varlet altogether, and never by any chance a reckless firebrand who comes bluffing his way single-handed into a den of lions."

Giles had begun to grin despite himself, for Colley's good nature was outrageously infectious. "Oh, aye," he conceded ruefully. " 'Tis what she always says. And doubtless I am an altogether pigeon-livered fellow—but at least I'm no rogue," he added bleakly, banishing his grin with a sense of having consorted with the enemy. "And that's a matter between Linnet and me, in any case. I want her back at once. Where is she?"

"Who?" asked Colley, bland as milk, his brown eyes dancing wickedly.

Giles turned scarlet, clenched his fists, and controlled himself with a truly heroic effort. It was increasingly clear that he was going to need all his wits this evening, and losing his temper would not sharpen them.

"Why fence about?" he demanded. "I know you've got her, and you know I know."

"Welladay." Colley sighed and shrugged ruefully. "I see Sparrow has badly underrated you. I don't suppose I could persuade you under any circumstances just to go away and forget the whole thing? No? I thought not. Ah well, then; come along into my study, and we'll talk about it." And he led the way up half a dozen stairs and through a wainscoted door.

Giles hesitated, and then with a mental shrug, followed. There were any number of traps he might be walking in to—but having already got to the heart of the lion's den, why jib now?

20

Out of the Lion's Den

Linnet sat in a despairing heap by the locked door, tears
rolling silently down her cheeks. Escape was impossible;
the top story overhung all the others, and the window presented only a sheer drop of three stories to the cobble-
stones below. It was all hopeless then: she and the Queen
were both doomed, and there was no help anywhere. If
only Giles. . . .

Almost at once there was a sound on the other side of
the door. Linnet shrank back in fear, and half scrambled to
her feet. It was the thing she had been fearing all along:
Colley had changed his mind and come back to silence her
here and now.

But the sound came again, and Linnet paused. For the
sound was faint and furtive, and surely there was a whispered argument going on outside the door?

A scratch on the door panel then. An urgent, frightened
whisper.

"Sparrow?"

The very caution made Linnet certain that, somehow,
help had come. "Yes?" she breathed, her mouth to the
crack. "Oh, let me out!"

In answer there was the grating of the heavy bolt, and then the door pushed slowly open to reveal a beaming Peace, momentarily forgetful of the dangers of the situation.

Nan hadn't forgotten. Her face was an odd cheesy color in the twilight of the corridor, and she shifted from one foot to the other in almost unbearable nervousness.

" 'E's still downstairs, Colley is," she whispered hoarsely. " 'Ow'll we get out? 'E's in the room where the tunnel comes out."

"Wiv Giles," added Peace with satisfaction.

Linnet stared. "Giles?" she echoed incredulously.

"Ar. 'E said 'e'd come for you, and Colley said come to 'is study to talk it over. And they did. And they're still there."

She was talking to air. Linnet, far more familiar with Over House than either Peace or Nan, was already whisking herself silently to the top of the stairs, to peer down at the hall below. Giles here? But how? How could he have found her? And how could he have walked into Colley's clutches that way? Why, he was as gullible as she had been! Wrath and alarm arose in her simultaneously as she peered down the stairs.

Gregory had lit the candles in the alcove of the landing, and they made small pools of yellow light surrounded by deep shadows. The rising wind drifted through the house in eddies, causing the flames to waver, and the tapestries to swing and ripple on the walls, and the shadows to sway, as if it were all under the sea. A tricky kind of light. It was extremely hard to tell whether anyone was in sight or not.

Linnet peered down for a long few moments, Nan breathing hard over her shoulder, and Peace at her elbow.

Nothing human stirred. Only wind and shadows and tapestries. Tapestries. . . . Linnet gave a sudden nod, touched Nan's arm, and wafted down the stairs like a wraith, followed by two thinner ghosts. They reached the bottom stair, paused for a moment, dark shapes among dark shapes, and drifted over to the wall nearest the study. The tapestry swung outward, rippled slightly, and settled itself again in its soft wind-blown dance. Only the sharpest eyes, looking for something odd, would have noticed the three girl-shapes in a still row behind it.

"Come come, my young fire-eater," said Colley. "Sit down, and have some claret, and tell me just what it is you think you know and how you learned it."

Giles refused the wine—more wisely than he knew, as Linnet could have told him—and concentrated on the verbal trap. He must not involve Salamon, whatever he did.

"I don't think I'll tell you everything," he said candidly, as he seated himself in a carved oaken chair opposite Colley. "Why should I? But I might point out that if you let her go wandering all over London with all that copper hair flying about, you ought not to be too surprised if someone recognizes her and follows her back."

Colley looked briefly annoyed, doubtless for having underestimated the opposition. Then he smiled again. "Welladay. And if I don't choose to return her?"

Even though Giles had contemplated this, he couldn't

help feeling angry and bewildered. "But—but, 'tis monstrous!" he stormed. "Anyway, what on earth could you possibly want with her? She's a perfect shatterwit."

"That's true," agreed Colley, apparently much struck by this.

"Then—then why are you keeping her, pray?"

"My dear Giles!" Colley shook a pitying head. "I'm a Rogue, by nature and by profession. Not a small rogue, mind, but a High Rogue, a Master Rogue. And when a charming and valuable pearl carefully arranges for no one to know where it is, and then obligingly drops itself into my pocket, you surely don't suppose I'd refuse it, do you? 'Twould be rank ingratitude."

Giles lowered his eyes, trying not to show that Colley had scored a hit. "To be sure," he murmured, between his teeth. "Indeed, I quite see. Still—" He found that he could look up with an air of dispassion. "Still, I wonder if you don't sometimes find that stolen pearls—even charming and valuable ones—turn out to be more trouble than they're worth?" He felt quite safe in guessing this. Unless Linnet had changed out of all comprehension, her independence of spirit must surely have disconcerted even a man like Colley.

Colley's eyes barely flickered. "Ah," he said. "There's the crux of the thing, of course. How much is a pearl worth? You see, my dear Giles, even aside from the ransom—I did mention ransom, didn't I? No? Lackaday! Well, aside from that, I felt that I could use her as a most opportune aid in a certain small bit of business I'd been working on. Well, she's served her purpose there, but

I'm not at all sure I want to let her go." He looked thoughtful. "Actually, I might say I'm quite certain that I don't. For one thing, she's an engaging little minx, and I might well decide to keep and train her to be my doxy some day." He grinned wickedly as Giles went scarlet. "She's promising, by my fay. More intelligent than she appears." He frowned. "In fact, rather too intelligent, I fear. She's been far too inquisitive, my young friend; a fault I see she shares with you. 'Tis pity—" He shook a regretful head and fell into deep reflection.

"What do you mean?" demanded Giles uneasily. He braced both arms on those of the carved oaken chair, ready for quick defense, but uncomfortably aware that his rapier was little more than a toy and that he had never used it in earnest; whereas Colley— "What's a pity?"

But Colley's smile was so warm, so merry, so ingenuous, that Giles felt a bit silly. "What? Oh, I was but saying 'tis a pity you two will go on complicating my life so abominably," he complained. Giles, quite disarmed by this, relaxed again. It was a mistake Linnet could have warned him about, but she was in no position to do so; and Colley went on, at his most charming. "Haply you're right, and I'd best give up the idea of keeping her, after all." He sighed, wistful. "Well, then, naught for it but to get the both of you out of my beard, eh? Wait you here, young Giles, whilst I go see about it."

It was not until the study door closed behind Colley and the key turned decisively in the lock that Giles realized there could be more than one way of taking that last remark.

It being too late for action, he sat still for an instant, the back of his neck prickling under his ruff. The air was suddenly more thick and stifling than ever under the burden of the building storm. Giles tried the door, with moist palms, just to make sure. It was indubitably, implacably locked, with the huge key, infuriatingly, left in the other side, blocking the keyhole. He could almost touch it with the tip of his little finger, but it might as well have been in Guildford for all the good it did him. He could neither push nor shake it loose.

He straightened, baffled, angry, incredulous, and deeply alarmed. What might be happening to Linnet this very minute, while he, like a greengoose, was trapped and helpless? The thought chilled him despite the heat that sent a trickle of perspiration down the inside of his ruff.

Silence. A rat scuttled somewhere behind the wainscoting and stopped again as the slow, heavy step of a man—probably Gregory—came by, paused, and went on again. More silence. More faint scrabbling. And then—the key moved in the lock.

Giles started, fingers on his rapier hilt. The key grated, stuck, turned with a clunk. Out of the shadows there appeared an indignant freckled face topped with copper hair. Finger to lips, it slipped into the room, followed by two girls whom Giles recognized at once. Ignoring him for the moment, Linnet closed the door softly behind her and locked it from the inside. "That should confuse him when he comes back," she observed with satisfaction. After which she turned and surveyed Giles for a long reproachful moment.

"Well, it's about time you came!" she told him tartly. "And now, would you like to be rescued by a perfect shatterwit?"

Giles subdued several strong impulses simultaneously.

The secret tunnel was having an extremely busy day. This time it was four figures who made the trip back from Over House to Nether House. It was risky, of course— but considerably less risky than anything else they could think of. And in any case, they had all four of them been doing so many hair-raising things that evening that they were getting quite used to being scared half out of their wits. Besides, as Giles pointed out hopefully, Colley was unlikely to use his secret door in front of his prisoner.

It occurred to him presently that a prisoner destined, alas, for an early grave might not require such caution. It was a disturbing idea, and one he thought it kinder not to mention to the girls—who, as it turned out, had thought of it even before he did. After all, they knew Colley quite a bit better than did Giles.

What with one thing and another, there was a distinct sense of urgency about their progress through the tunnel, and a wary look in their eyes as they stood at last peering out into the blind passage in Nether House.

Dim and muffled from the common room came the murmur of voices, almost as if this were just any summer evening with no storm brewing other than in the sky. They were almost safe, now: there was just the problem of getting to the front door and then out of Slops Alley without meeting any of the Flock coming home.

"C'm on!" breathed Peace, wanting to get it over. Linnet nodded. Giles, knowing nothing about Nether House, could only hope that the girls knew what they were doing. Hearts beating hard, they tiptoed forward through the maze toward the front door—and the front door screeched open.

They froze, only one corner between them and the light swift footsteps that the girls instantly recognized as Colley's. Down the other corridor he moved, toward the common room.

"Ho, goslings!" rang his cheerful voice. "Ho, Diggory, Joan! I have—Diggory?" His voice faded into a sudden babble, not unlike goslings, at that. Cockney goslings. Giles could scarce understand a word. But Colley's voice was clear enough.

"Really?" he said, after a moment of the babble. "Wella-day!"

In the dark of the narrow maze, four pairs of hands clutched at one another tensely, while Maudlin's voice in the common room murmured alone.

"I see." Colley's voice sounded lazy, amused, dangerous. There was a brief but interminable silence. Then his foot-steps came back, along the passage to the front door, which groaned open and thudded shut. Giles started to move, but Linnet, wise by now in Colley's wiles, clutched his sleeve in warning. The silence held. The sound of voices arose again in the common room. Slowly four pairs of lungs in the dark maze began to breathe again.

And the next time the front door groaned and thudded, no one came in.

21

Tell It to Walsingham

Hugh ambled along the Strand toward Ludgate, grumbling to himself. It seemed he was doomed to spend his life hunting either for Giles's red-haired runaway who probably deserved never to be found, or else for Giles himself. Or both. Life was too short and too complicated. For there was also his own problem, still unsolved. Every time he decided it was his plain duty to tell his father the things Amy Throckmorton had hinted at, he found himself tongue-tied by Lord Crowden's worried, preoccupied air.

He sighed again as he neared the eastern end of Fleet Street and the London wall loomed ahead. That was the trouble with life, in a nutshell. Much too complicated.

Almost instantly it became even more so. A group of extremely disreputable young people was swarming out Ludgate toward him. Hugh didn't at all like their looks, and suddenly wished he had brought his bodyguard. As he regarded them with wary disfavor, he found his eyes fixing themselves particularly on a vacant-faced, hulking young man whom he had surely seen before. And the girl with brassy hair and a birthmark on her cheek, too. . . . He remembered where. They had gone into that house. The one he could never find again. The one where Linnet had gone. Fate, it seemed, was presenting him with a second chance.

Hugh muttered something unkind about Fate. Then, as the group drew abreast of him, he sighed and did his duty.

"Look here," he said, addressing them impartially. "What have you done with young Linnet?"

The effect was truly remarkable. The entire group stopped short and fixed him with an assortment of beady eyes that made his spine crawl. He instinctively reached down to his belt to protect his pocket, and just in time. A small hand slithered away from his touch, and a small voice hissed an obscenity in tones of deep annoyance.

Joan, as always, took the initiative. " 'Oo are you?" she demanded aggressively. "Wot d'yer know abaht Sparrow?"

Hugh looked justifiably confused. "Not Sparrow; Linnet. A girl with red hair and a funny eyebrow."

"That's 'er," said the Flock comfortably. "We calls 'er Sparrow." They exchanged glances, suspicious by instinct and training of all gentry coves. " 'Ow d'yer know we knows 'er?"

"I saw some of you with her not a fortnight ago," returned Hugh. He looked severe. " 'Tis monstrous, you know. Keeping her, I mean. Giles has been in a vile distemper, trying to find her, and half the gentry in Westminster are laughing at him."

More looks were exchanged. This gentry cove might be useful, at that. " 'Er's told us all abaht Giles," said Diggory affably. " 'Oo are you, then? 'Ermes? Can't be 'Eracles," he informed the others. "Too capsy."

"I'm Giles's friend," said Hugh impatiently, annoyed at

being discussed and cross-examined in this casual manner when he should be the one asking the questions. "Giles has been staying with me. My father, I mean. Lord Crowden. And I'm looking for Giles now, and he's off somewhere looking for Linnet. What have you done with her?"

They ignored this last question. "Lord Crowden?" echoed Joan. "A real lord? Coo! 'Ere, Bet, give 'im 'is purse back! And you, Jack; keep your fambles off 'is shoe buckles. Look 'ere, young sir, us 'as got ter see the Queen. Or at least Walsingham," she amended reasonably.

"Eh?" Hugh's face was a study.

" 'Tis a Papist plot," said Peg, coming to the heart of the thing.

This produced the most gratifying attention. "Plot?" bleated Hugh. He grabbed the nearest arm with an amazing disregard for the insect life doubtless inhabiting it. "Plot!" He shoved his face close. "What plot?"

Everyone talked at once. It took a full five minutes of jabbering and slow translation of thieves' cant into English before Hugh managed to get a clear picture in his mind. Faced with another decision, he grappled manfully for a moment before it dawned on him that there was a logical solution which would also solve his own dilemma.

"Come tell my father about it," he said with sudden decision, and began to lead the way back toward the Strand. He felt rather like a modern Sixteenth Century version of the Pied Piper—but oddly sure of himself for a change, and not even seriously disconcerted at his extraordinary company.

The Flock, like a comet's tail, trailed behind, chattering light-heartedly. Everything was all right. Now, they told each other, the Queen would be saved, and Colley never know a thing about their part in it. It was a pity about Sparrow, of course; they'd miss her sorely. But that was life, wasn't it? The odds were against any of them living to a ripe old age, and really, it was only the Queen who mattered.

When they reached Crowden House, Hugh, struck by a belated sense of caution, suggested that they all wait outside while he went in to his father. They hooted. Not they, they assured him. They'd just stick close and make sure the Queen got the warning—and, just incidentally, that they got the reward sure to be presented for such loyal service.

Hugh sighed and didn't argue. Bearing with resignation and some dignity the astonished glances of the servants, he commanded curtly that these—er—young persons should wait in the entry hall. And before Joan could protest, he shrewdly selected her to go with him to see his father. He knew quite well what he was doing. Let her be the one to tell Father what was going on among his Throckmorton kinfolk.

Joan did so, unabashed by the richness of her surroundings. It was a pity Sparrow hadn't had the chance to blab a bit more before Colley came in, but there it was. But it was enough, surely, to come crab on the Papist plotters and save Queen Bess. . . . Lord Crowden, she noted, was wearing a rather odd expression by the time she'd finished.

"Holy Mother of God!" he said simply, and turned to stare out the window into the murky dusk.

Joan stared. " 'Ere!" she exclaimed in alarm. "That's wot Papists say!" She looked accusingly at Hugh. "Why didn't yer tell me? Tricked us, yer did!" And she turned in panic to leave. But Lord Crowden paid no attention whatever, and Hugh merely told her impatiently not to be such a fool; so she thought better of it, and waited curiously until His Lordship turned around again.

He looked suddenly much older than he had. "Aye, we'd best to Walsingham," he said in a perfectly ordinary voice. "Did you say, Son, that you had several more— er—guests—waiting below?"

Hugh nodded. "If the hall's still there at all," he mused pessimistically. "I warrant they've pocketed even the tapestries and footmen by now. They picked my pocket at least three times on the way here, and even filched my shoe buckles; and only gave them back because this girl and a tall fellow they call Diggory said something in that heathenish cant—"

"Said you be cully even if you are a flash cove," Joan informed him in tones of aggrieved virtue. "And Diggory said as 'e'd douse the glims of any weevily scab wot prigged you again. 'E never said nuffin' about your 'ouse, though," she pointed out cheerfully, "so belike you're right abaht the 'all." Her brow furrowed as she realized she'd had no opportunity at the entry hall, and the others would have got everything long before now. Always sensible and foresighted about such things, she at once helped herself to a fine silver-filigree pouncet box, bejeweled and enameled, that lay conveniently on the table. Neither Lord Crowden nor his son saw a thing. In any case, their attention was distracted by what was probably going on downstairs.

"'Swounds!" said Lord Crowden, and hurried down, Hugh behind him. Joan, bringing up the rear, found ample opportunity to collect a nice little candle-snuffer in passing.

Below, the rest of the Flock stood staring around at the rich entry hall with wide eyes, and making candid comments about the servants, who stood watching with nervous alertness.

" 'Is Lordship's going ter take us ter Walsing'am," Joan informed them, noting with satisfaction that the rich hall was considerably less rich than it had been.

Hugh noticed as well, and had a burst of brilliance, based partly on his experience of the past half hour. "Aye," he said affably. "And it might be awkward, mark you, if any—er—prigged loot—were found on you in front of the Secretary of State and Head of Secret Service, so I think you'd best put everything back at once, and say you were just practicing." And he grinned at them good-naturedly, much to everyone's surprise—including his own. But he was so relieved at being out of his personal dilemma that he was willing to make allowances for anyone, even these appalling young thieves from the dregs of the social order.

The Flock turned saintly innocent gazes upon him. The servants looked reproachful. Was he accusing them of carelessness?

"We've been watching them every instant, Master Hugh," said the head footman, pained. "They haven't touched a thing, I vow."

Hugh raised a skeptical eyebrow and grinned at Joan, who scowled, looked virtuous, and then shrugged and grinned back.

" 'Ere you are, young flash cove," she said, producing the pouncet box and candle-snuffer, and enjoying his startled face. The others, reluctantly following her lead, turned out a score of small objects, some of which had been on the very persons of the servants, who looked deeply chagrined.

"Mind," said Joan, cuffing young Jack to encourage compliance, "we'll be 'aving a good reward, we will." And turning back to Hugh, she exclaimed, "C'mon, then; wot are we waiting for?"

They set out for Whitehall.

Hugh wondered afterwards whether the covey of ragged and unprepossessing street urchins would ever have got in to see Walsingham had they been alone. On the whole he rather thought they would, for they came armed with that magic password: *Papist Plot*. With that and the dignified and well-known presence of Lord Crowden, they were instantly ushered into a rich anteroom where they waited such a short time that they never got around to prigging a thing. So when, presently, they faced Sir Francis Walsingham, it was with faces of genuine if temporary innocence.

He was still at work, late though it was. He sat behind a heavy oaken table covered with documents, reports, and lists, flanked by two overworked secretaries and two armed guards. The richly somber room was lit well but fitfully by sconces of tall wax candles that flickered with every gust of warm wind through the tall open casements. Outside, above a shadowed garden, the summer dusk was darkening with unnatural rapidity. A pile of thunderheads obscured the setting sun and shot out little tongues of lightning, and thunder grumbled an accompaniment. Sir Francis raised deep-set eyes, surveyed the peculiarly ill-assorted group with keen appraisal, and then fixed his attention on Hugh and his father with brooding intensity.

Hugh shuffled his feet uncomfortably. Who would ever have thought that he, a loyal Roman Catholic, would of his own free will stand here facing the arch Anti-Papist himself? For Sir Francis was known to hate Popery with a fanatical hatred that went back ten years: to 1572, when he had had the misfortune to be in Paris at the time of the dreadful massacre of St. Bartholomew. Thousands of men, women, and children were butchered ruthlessly, and very few Protestants doubted that both Spain and the Pope had been in on the plan from the beginning, nor that they intended the same sort of thing for England. And although this conviction put Sir Francis into direct opposition with Queen Elizabeth's extraordinary policy of religious tolerance, it also made him the best possible watchdog for the Queen's life.

"Well?" he asked dryly of Lord Crowden.

Hugh's father clearly felt as uncomfortable as did Hugh, but he maintained a grave dignity that made Hugh proud of him. "These—er—youths, or the wench here, actually, have just told me of a new plot against Her Majesty. I know nothing of it, personally, nor whether it be true or not; but I judged it my duty to bring them to you at once."

There was a short hard silence between the two men, like duelers testing each others' mettle for the first time. Clearly Sir Francis had a dark suspicious nature that saw treachery in every Papist, and considered this most likely to be an extremely clever and subtle new kind of trick. His eyes moved to Hugh, who flushed but met them straight.

"I know what you're thinking," he blurted resentfully, "but it isn't true."

A wintry smile flickered across Sir Francis' lean face, and his attention moved on to the Flock, who were bunched together for courage, and trying to work themselves up to their normal state of cockiness. "Tell me about it, then," he said, his voice surprisingly kind.

Joan, of course, elected herself spokesman, flanked by Diggory and Peg. Hugh subdued a wry grin as the broad Cockney flowed forth, liberally laced with thieves' cant. He could hardly understand two words in five, himself.

"Colley's a coney-catcher, see, 'n 'twas 'e twigged it, when 'e got cully with this Papist gentry cove and 'is family, wot thought Colley was a flash cove too, see: that was 'is lay. So 'e let 'em convert 'im to a Papist—only not really, you know—and took Sparrow along as 'is daughter to be friends with their dell, and be converted, too, 'cos 'er really is a gentry mort, see: Sparrow, I mean. None of us could've talked right," she admitted modestly. "Not even me. So anyway, the Papist dell's a havey-cavey peagoose wot squeaked beef ter Sparrow about this Enterprise, see, and—"

"This what?" Walsingham, who seemed to be having remarkably little difficulty with the language barrier, leaned forward suddenly, his eyes sharper than ever in his austere face. "What did you call it?"

Joan looked uncertain. "Sparrow called it that. Something like The Enterprise, any'ow . . . didn't she?" She looked at the others, and they nodded solemn support. Sir Francis flicked a swift commanding glance at the secretary on his left, who, in fact, was already reaching for a sheaf of closely-written documents. This he proceeded to hunt through with the air of a hound who has at last caught sight of the fox.

Walsingham turned back to Joan. "Go on," he said encouragingly.

"Ar, well," said Joan. "The Enterprise is a new plot ter do in our Queen 'n prig 'er crown 'n give England ter the Pope."

"Yes, yes, girl; but the details? Who, and when, and how?"

" 'At's all us knows," Joan told him, crestfallen. " 'S Colley 'n Sparrow knows all about it. Sparrow only told us a bit."

Really, Walsingham could look very grim indeed. Hugh, now well on the left side of the room, near the casements (for the Flock was distinctly odorous in a closed room), was glad those eyes weren't on him.

"Why didn't they come to me, then, instead of sending you?"

The Flock shuffled their feet slightly. They looked at one another. They sighed a little with a strong air of wishing themselves somewhere else. But Walsingham's eyes were compelling, and Diggory at last spoke.

" 'E was going to," he explained. "But 'e 'adn't got round to it yet. 'Ad a bit of business wiv the Papists, see. Make a bit of profit, like. 'E 'as ter make a livin', yer know," he added reasonably. "So 'e told 'em 'e'd twigged their lay 'n they'd 'ave ter fork over some rhino or 'e'd

squeak beef. They're Papists, see." Clearly this made anything anyone did to them all right. "Only—" He dried up
suddenly, and Joan took over the difficult bit.

"See, we—well, 'twas takin' a mort of time, see, and
—uh—"

Walsingham came to her rescue. "And you came along
to me because you feared it might slip his mind altogether?" he suggested, his manner sympathetic now.

"Ar," she agreed. " 'At's it. 'E's absent-minded, like,
Colley is, see." She looked at the others, who instantly
backed this up.

"Abaht some fings, any'ow," they amended honestly,
and then peered anxiously to see how Walsingham would
receive this information.

He nodded. "Aye; just so. Many people are, I've noticed. Important matters of . . . business and profit do tend
to . . . dominate the attention."

His irony was lost on them. They sighed and smiled
happily.

"And what about this other person? This Sparrow?"

Pained silence. Furtive and abashed glances were exchanged, and bare feet shuffled silently on the clean rushes.
They'd like to help Sparrow, of course, but was this possible without squeaking on Colley? Probably not. In any
case, it was doubtless too late for Sparrow.

But Walsingham was fixing them with his eagle stare,
sharp and demanding and hypnotic. "Don't you love your
Queen, after all?" he asked them, undertones of danger in
his voice. "Come, tell me; where is this Sparrow you mentioned?"

" 'Er's scrobbled," blurted young Jack, breaking under

the threat. "Cocked up 'er toes by now. Colley 'eard 'er blabbin' 'n took 'er off. That's why we come," he confessed simply, abandoning pretense.

There was a brief but stunned silence in the stifling room as the meaning of this sank in.

"Sparrow?" Hugh croaked. "But that's Linnet! Giles's Linnet, that he's been hunting all over London for; the one with red hair and a funny eyebrow. You mean she's killed?" His voice rose to a horrified squeak, and he glared across the room at the Flock, aghast.

They nodded sheepishly, clearly most unhappy over the whole thing.

Lord Crowden wore the shocked look of a man struck down, and Walsingham half rose from his chair and reached for a bell on his table, which he rang violently. An armed servant instantly rushed in.

"The guard!" snapped Sir Francis. "A score of men, armed, at the gate in one minute's time." He turned to the quaking Flock. "One of you will guide them."

The Flock stared. "Who?" they asked. "Where?"

"To wherever this Colley and Sparrow are likely to be. You know more about it than I do; use your judgment. Do you want to save the Queen or don't you?" he hissed as they hesitated.

Polly took a deep breath and stepped forward. Joan nodded.

" 'Strewf," she said. "You'll want two, then; one for Over 'Ouse and one for Nether 'Ouse. Jack, you'll go, too."

In a matter of seconds Polly and Jack were ushered out under the lowering sky where twenty armed guards, still adjusting swords and cloaks, hurried into formation. And silence reigned in Walsingham's chamber, broken presently by a sharp gust of wind and a guard closing the casement. Hugh swallowed, feeling ill. Poor Giles!

The eyes of Lord Crowden and Sir Francis met, haunted and appalled. Hugh, with unusual perspicacity, saw the mutual mistrust melt for a moment as each of them recognized in the other a man of sincerity, doing his best to choose right among all the possible wrongs.

22

Confrontation

It was lovely, squabbling with Giles again. They did it all the way across London and down Fleet Street, alternately scolding each other and telling each other their adventures, and arguing about what they should have done and ought to do and what was going to happen now. They were followed in fascinated silence by Nan and Peace, and Salamon, who had seen them at the corner of Slops Alley and at once attached himself.

"Well, I'm not at all sure I like the way you went around describing me," Linnet grumbled as they went through Ludgate. "Still, it was clever of you to track me down that way; I doubt anyone else could have done it."

"I doubt anyone else would have been dolt enough to want to," Giles informed her disagreeably.

"But all the same, when Mistress Throckmorton practically told you about me, you—"

"She didn't. She just said Amy's friend Jennet had apricot hair."

Linnet tossed the apricot hair in question. "Well, you should have known it was me."

"You? A Papist convert with a different name and a

strange father? Besides, Mistress Throckmorton had seen still another apricot-haired girl, in Chepeside."

"That was me, too," Linnet informed him triumphantly. "I remember: she was staring out her litter at me, and I turned my back just in time. . . . I suppose you do know where we're going?" she added in tones suggesting that she wasn't at all sure.

Peace emerged from an unnaturally long silence. "Ter tell Walsing'am about the plot, blubber'ead!" she bawled from behind.

"Well, naturally," snapped Linnet. "But where? Does anybody know where to find him?"

There was a disconcerted silence.

"Whitehall," remembered Salamon. "All 'Er Majesty's Court lives at Whitehall, don't they?"

"Well, that's what I mean," said Linnet. "That's an awful lot of people, isn't it? And Whitehall's monstrous big, isn't it? And I don't think it would be very practical just to go wandering around hoping he'll come bumping into us and introduce himself; do you, Giles?"

She peered up at Giles sideways and saw him smother a grin. It was all right, then; he knew where to go. She gave a small skip of contentment. Thunder growled overhead. She frowned up at the looming clouds and gave vent to the thought that had been haunting them all—or at least four of them—all the way from Slops Alley.

"I wonder where Colley is, and if he's found us gone yet, and what he'll do about it when he does."

Nan shuddered, preferring not to think about it. Giles, whose knowledge of Colley was still young, looked mildly surprised.

"Who cares?"

Salamon and the girls exchanged meaningful glances. Salamon put their feelings in a nutshell.

"Coo!" he said simply.

The sky was even darker as they reached the Strand, and thunder rumbled with a nearer and more businesslike sound. By the time they reached the village of Charing Cross, there were few others on the street, and those few hurrying for shelter with uneasy glances upward. Only the group of liveried guards who came toward them with two shabby figures who resembled—well, almost. . . . Seized with a spirit of mischief, Linnet turned her head.

"Isn't that Polly and Jack with those soldiers?" she suggested to the goslings behind.

Nan at once squeaked with alarm, but Peace and Salamon hooted.

"Walking with soldier coves? Think they're betwaddled or somefing?"

But before Linnet's appreciative giggle reached her lips, the skies opened. There was a shattering explosion of thunder, and even as they flinched from it, they were blinded, battered, and drenched by an avalanche of rain. Visibility reduced itself to inches, and surely it was sheer lunacy not to get under the nearest doorway.

But then, while they hesitated, a score of dim shapes slogged determinedly past, heads down against the deluge, heading toward London. Giles set his teeth. If those soldiers could carry on, then he was certainly not going to cry quits! He looked at Linnet, who grinned recklessly and nodded. Why not, since they couldn't possibly get any wetter than they were already? Teeth set, they pressed on against the storm, around the river bend, and southward to Whitehall.

Whitehall Palace was indeed enormous. The rain was easing now, and Linnet's eyes widened at the rambling pile of it, covering twenty-four acres: the largest palace in Christendom, said Giles, as he led them to the turreted gateway.

The guards on each side were feeling wet and steamy and bad-tempered. They looked sourly at Giles, who, looking and sounding more confident than he felt, strode up and demanded to be taken to Walsingham.

The taller guard looked down his nose. Sir Francis, he informed them, was—along with Lord Burleigh—the Queen's most important minister: he hadn't time to see every Tom, Dick, or Harry at all times of night.

" 'Sooth," agreed Giles, with an air that caused both guards to look at him again. The sodden clothes this young man was wearing were those of a gentleman, however dubious those ragamuffins with him. "Don't be officious," Giles went on rather snappishly. "You know as well as I do that Sir Francis Walsingham is always available to those who bear word of—" He paused dramatically before intoning the magic password. "—of a Papist Plot."

"Oh," said the taller guard weakly. This was true. It was also true that by now everyone in England must know that password—but it was not, thank goodness, a mere Yeoman's duty to sort out the frauds. He sighed and called for the Captain of the Guard, who set the proper wheels in motion, and in a short time word of their names and errand had been sent to the Secretary of State and spoken privately in his ear. Back came a forceful answer, and in an even shorter time, Giles and party were ushered into Walsingham's chamber.

There was a stupified silence when the dripping quintet appeared in the doorway. Giles broke it first.

"I told you I'd find her in London," he observed, looking at Hugh and his father. "But what are you—"

He was interrupted by Peg, who let out a wail expressing the convictions of the other goslings. "Ow, 'tis 'er ghost!"

Linnet was staring at them with pleased astonishment. "Oh, you came! I'm so glad! I should have known you'd never leave the Queen in the nitch."

There was a brief silence while the Flock stared at Linnet, and then everyone turned to look at Walsingham. But he was getting his information merely by sitting in silence absorbing every sound and gesture and expression. They all looked back at one another, and Linnet giggled.

That decided the Flock.

"You ain't cocked up your toes," decided Joan, incredulous. "But—'ow'd yer get away from Colley?"

"Us saved 'er!" shouted Peace brashly from behind. "Nan 'n me! 'N then all of us saved Giles, and—"

"Giles!" yelped the Flock, fascinated. "Coo, izzat Giles then?"

Linnet ignored them and turned directly to Sir Francis. "I'm Linnet Seymour, Sir. Have Joan and the others told you all about The Enterprise?"

"Not quite all," he said with admirable restraint. "Only that it exists, in point of fact. Am I to gather that you're

commonly known as Sparrow?" Everyone nodded. "Yes.
Well, I don't suppose you and Master Campion here happened to run into an unfortunate party out looking for
you? No? Never mind. I warrant they'll find their way
back eventually—perhaps bringing this Colley, whom I
should very much like to meet." (The Flock looked horrified at this idea; particularly Nan, Peace, and Salamon,
who began glancing around the room for possible exits and
hiding places.) "Now, if you can spare a few moments,
Mistress Linnet-Sparrow, do you think you might enlighten me regarding this Enterprise? I've been wondrous
patient, I think, but I am a busy man, and have not yet had
my supper, and what with one interruption after another
I—"

At that moment there was another interruption.

It took the form of Colley. He strolled in, unannounced
and with a spluttering doorman in his wake, as noncha-
lantly as if he owned the place. Pausing for a splendid and
sweeping bow to Sir Francis, he then turned to gaze at the
quaking Flock with affable interest. For the moment he
quite overlooked Giles and Linnet, who were over by the
window and behind the portly Lord Crowden and Hugh.
And Linnet, like the stricken Flock, felt a strong desire to
be invisible. Was Colley in league with Satan, after all? To
sweep in like this—and with only half a dozen splotches
of rain marring the fine sky-blue of his cloak.

Then she pulled herself together. Not magic: just Colley. He was dry because he had taken shelter from the
rain. And this explained how it was that he left Nether
House a few minutes before them, and arrived now, a few

minutes after them. His vanity wouldn't have permitted him to appear before Walsingham dripping and drenched, and besides, that would weaken the effect he would make. And he had known that he needed to come here and create a good effect, because Maudlin had undoubtedly told him where Joan and her cronies had gone, and why. And this meant he had come straight here. He had not had time to stop back at Over House, and therefore he must be suffering from the pleasant delusion that she and Giles were still in captivity there.

Odd how quickly thoughts happened. It had been only a moment since Colley strode in. He was still bending a genial eye on the dismayed Flock.

"There's my good loyal goslings," he purred, to their great confusion. "You've done just as I wished, to help save our beloved Queen. But as you see, 'tis all right: the Papist plotters didn't manage to kill or imprison me, so I can tell Sir Francis about the plot, myself." And he turned to the waiting Walsingham with a look of such shattering virtue that one could almost see his halo. "Have they told you aught yet?"

"They have told me there's a new Papist plot which they call The Enterprise," said that gentleman guardedly. "I knew this much already. We stopped a spy trying to cross the Scottish border, some weeks ago, in May. He carried concealed letters that referred to it. Now what else have you to add?"

But Colley was no longer listening. He had seen Linnet and Giles.

His face didn't change, but for an instant his eyes went

blank with shock—and in that instant Linnet felt repaid for everything. She and Giles had Colley in a forked stick, and he knew it.

"We just thought we'd come along, too," Giles said. "In case the wicked Papists locked you up in a room or something."

Colley all but flinched. Then he rallied. He was a sportsman if nothing else, and would play the game to the end —and play to win at any odds, too. The three of them smiled urbanely at one another, while Sir Francis watched with deep interest.

Then Colley turned his smile to include Walsingham. "Welladay; to business, then," he suggested boldly. "We mustn't waste any more of Sir Francis's valuable time. Have you told him all about everything, then?"

It was the key question, double-edged. And not knowing how much had been told, he couldn't know that everyone in the room perceived it. Nor did Giles and Linnet choose to enlighten him.

"Not yet," they said in unison, and with equally double meaning.

"I see," said Colley thoughtfully, and did. He stroked his beard and regarded them with new respect. He had, it seemed, made the mistake of underestimating them, and if there's anything more dangerous than overrating one's own intelligence, it's underrating that of one's opponent. Giles and Linnet didn't make that error.

"You tell him all about it," Linnet urged Colley. "You'll do it much better than we could."

It was a neat trap. But before Colley could fall or be pushed into it, Lord Crowden interrupted. "Wait!" he said unhappily. "Before anyone tells anything, my son and I will take our leave. We know no more about this plot than has been told already, and to be candid, we don't want to. We've done our duty in coming to you; now let's be quit of the whole matter."

Walsingham narrowed his eyes. "You don't want to know who is involved, then? They are like to be friends of yours, you know."

"Quite," said Lord Crowden stiffly. " 'Twould put me in an intolerable position."

"Conflict of loyalties," murmured Sir Francis, looking sardonic and not particularly sympathetic. He knew no such conflicts. "You might, I gather, be tempted to drop a warning into the right ear. But then, a word to any Papist would almost certainly reach the right ear, whether you know which it is, or not. How am I to know you won't drop that word at random?" He looked icy and implacable suddenly, and Linnet shivered, not for the first time that warm evening. Suspected traitors were tortured; that was accepted custom. Was Lord Crowden in danger of this?

He was, and he knew it; she could tell by the steady way he returned Sir Walsingham's stare. "You must use your own judgment," he said simply. There was another long pause while the two pairs of eyes met, and while Linnet realized fully that some Papists had courage and loyalty and nobility of spirit. . . .

"Go, then," said Walsingham irritably, and Lord Crowden did so, pausing only to inform Giles that a bedchamber would be prepared for Mistress Linnet, and an armed servant sent to meet them outside Whitehall Palace and escort them home. Then he and Hugh left, and Walsingham stared after them with grudging respect. "Now, my man." He turned to Colley. "Am I to have that information at last?"

Colley had had time to think. "Aye, heartily, Sir," he said, and with one swift mischievous twinkle at Linnet and Giles, he turned to the impatient spymaster.

And with scrupulous candor he told about The Enterprise.

Just the plot, of course. Why not? It was all Walsingham had asked for, all he cared about. He listened with the look of a hawk watching its dinner, pouncing now and then with a penetrating question. At last, when Colley stopped, Sir Francis turned to Linnet.

"Any additions or corrections?"

Linnet glared at Colley, who looked like a cat in the cream. "You haven't mentioned why it was you didn't report the plot as soon as you found out about it, you know."

Walsingham nodded interestedly, but Colley just chuckled. "You want me to confess that I wished first to make them pay me for not telling what I'd learned," he said. "Very well, I do confess it: 'tis exactly why I waited."

"You mean," asked Giles carefully, "you accepted these people's hospitality, lied to them, blackmailed them, and then informed on them?"

Colley looked hurt. "They're Papists," he pointed out reasonably.

Walsingham clearly agreed. But Linnet couldn't let it go. Fair was fair.

"You can't judge all Papists by a few!" she cried. "Anyway, that doesn't justify your treachery; ethics don't work that way. If—"

She stopped. Walsingham's brooding dark eyes were fixed on her. Giles, startled and alarmed, moved to stand squarely beside Linnet, because he agreed with her completely, and because he would have defended her even if Walsingham hadn't.

"Mmm," Walsingham said finally, and changed the subject. "Tell me, my man, just what were you planning to do with Mistress Seymour and Master Campion once you'd collected your money from the plotters?"

"Oh, they've told you I locked them up, have they?" said Colley merrily. He seemed not to notice the sudden self-conscious movement from the silent Flock. His face glowed with candor and rueful humor. "What a trial they've been, to be sure! Why, I planned to keep them safely behind locked doors until I'd seen you," he confessed, unabashed. "After all, why should they have the —er—credit—when all the genius, organization, and hard work was mine?"

Giles and Linnet looked at each other, speechless. Linnet opened her mouth. Then she closed it again. Giles took a deep breath and then shrugged. Colley had outmaneuvered them after all, in the easiest and most obvious way imaginable. They knew what was coming next.

"Surely they didn't think I offered them any threat?"

He hadn't, of course. Any more than he had threatened Throckmorton, in so many words. Linnet felt her face go scarlet with indignation.

"You said—you said—"

"What did he say?" asked Walsingham, apparently not unwilling to find good cause for hanging Colley once his usefulness was over.

"That he wouldn't throw me in the Thames before dark or have me for supper," she muttered sheepishly. Giles gave her a disgusted look, Colley laughed aloud, and even Sir Francis almost smiled. She sighed and gave it up. She didn't know what he'd intended, there wasn't a single thing she could prove against him, and she wasn't really sure she wanted to, after all. Though he was a rogue who undoubtedly deserved hanging any number of times over, Linnet found the idea distasteful.

So did Giles. Helplessly they began to laugh.

Walsingham abruptly lost interest in all of them. He had got what he wanted. "Go!" he said, waving them out. Then he pointed at Colley. "You will be under surveillance from now on, so I should advise you and your—er—goslings to be extremely careful. Give ye good den."

Outside, the darkness was broken by torches at every gate to Whitehall, and by the half-moon blinking from between scattering clouds. Two guards in the Crowden livery awaited Giles and Linnet, but they paused. There was unfinished business.

They all looked at one another uncertainly: Linnet and Giles, the Flock, even Colley. But the awkward moment was bridged by the ever practical Joan.

"Wot about the reward?" she squawked. "Colley, yer forgot ter ask 'im for the reward!"

Colley looked shocked. "Reward! Why, goslings, would

you ask a reward for doing our simple patriotic duty?"

They nodded. They'd serve the Queen in any case, of course, but they'd much sooner have a reward for it.

"Fie, for shame!" cried Colley, undoubtedly aware that at least two Yeomen of the Guard were listening with interest. "Have you forgotten all I've ever taught you?"

They looked confused. They remembered perfectly well all he had taught them. That was the trouble. Linnet giggled.

"Welladay," said Colley, and steered the unwieldy group a little further from the gate. "Welladay." He fingered his ruff as if it had suddenly turned into a noose. "To tell the truth," he admitted with an endearing frankness, "even my temerity has its limits. I'll settle for a whole skin now and find my reward later."

Linnet and Giles had no doubt that he would. And Linnet, crazily, found herself wishing just a tiny bit that she could be there to see it. But it was all over for her. Walsingham had been warned; the Queen would be saved from yet another assassination attempt; and Giles had rescued and been rescued by her. Presently they would go back to Guildford, where, with any luck, she could wheedle him and her godparents not to worry her family by squeaking beef. . . . Oh dear, she must stop using thieves' cant!

Suddenly, ordinary language seemed flavorless. The future looked dull. She was, she discovered with astonishment, going to miss the Flock, and even Colley.

Colley it was who now delayed the farewells. He was looking around at them all rather grimly. He smiled at Linnet and Giles. "Oh, by the way." His voice was like brown velvet. "Who did let you out?"

There was a short anguished silence. Nan, who had stuck like a burr to Linnet's left flank, clutched harder. Peace, fixed like a limpet to her right flank, pressed closer. Linnet felt herself blushing again, for shame. Selfish pig that she was, she had completely forgotten about them— and after they'd risked everything for her, too!

Salamon broke the silence. "Them done it," he announced, pointing a dirty forefinger, secure in the knowledge that his own betrayal of Colley was known only to Giles, who had sworn not to tell. And gentry coves, poor things, had to keep their word.

Colley seemed unsurprised. "I thought as much," he said sorrowfully. "Naughty goslings; where is your loyalty?"

Giles choked. Colley ignored him. "I've carefully trained you all; do you let me down?" He sighed. "Aye, you do," he decided. "You put the Queen before me. I shall have to speak to you about that one day. Still, that's forgivable. . . . But you!" He glared at the two culprits. "You gave your first loyalty not to me, nor even to the Queen, but to Sparrow! It won't do, goslings. It won't do at all. 'Tis a pity. . . . Nan's worthless, to be sure, but Peace held great promise." Clearly in his mind they were as good as dead already. He shook his dark head sadly. "I cast you out," he declared. "You are from this moment no more members of my Flock."

Nan moaned, but Peace jutted out her chin defiantly. And Linnet smiled.

"Good," she said. "That's most excellent; I'll just take them home with me."

"Cock's bones!" said Giles feelingly.

Colley's jaw dropped. For once—for the first and last

time in her life—Linnet saw him thoroughly and completely at a loss. Then he recovered himself, bowed as deeply as he had at their first meeting, and swept his plumed hat to the ground. "My felicitations, Mistress Sparrow," he murmured gravely. "Your parents will be delighted. Present them with my compliments, will you?"

"Cock's bones!" said Giles again.

Colley smiled, a little ruefully, ignoring Giles now. He touched Linnet's wayward eyebrow with his fingertip. "Fare ye well, Sparrow. You'd have made a fine doxy. . . ."

Giles found his tongue. "Wouldn't do at all," he said firmly. "She'd never make a doxy; she's far too independent. The fact is, you're still underestimating her, Colley, and you'd go on doing it, and just think you what that could lead to! One needs practice at not underestimating Linnet. And I," he pointed out with the air of one who knows his own worth, "have had more practice than almost anyone."

" 'Strewth," admitted Colley regretfully. "Well, then—"

"*Awaah!*" bawled Peace in a howl of anguish that caused people for a hundred yards in all directions to spin around. "PURSE-EFFONY! I want Purse-Effony!"

"God's bodkins!" roared Colley above the din. "Stubble it, you horrible child! You shall have the little monster." The screams stopped as if by magic, and Colley smiled wickedly at Giles's dismayed face. "Some of the Flock shall deliver it tomorrow, at Lord Crowden's house," he promised. "And now, fare ye well."

"Oh, not forever," said Linnet happily. "You'll see us again. Because think of all the changes that must be made!

And Giles and I are planning to start seeing about them just as soon as ever we can, aren't we, Giles? We'll begin by finding honest jobs for the Flock, and perhaps start a school for them, and—"

"Lackaday!" said Colley, stricken.

About the Author

Sally Watson was born in Seattle, Washington, and was graduated from Reed College in Oregon. Her home is now in Hampshire, England, where she combines writing with her other varied activities. Along with teaching judo (she has her brown belt) she also enjoys fencing and Highland dancing.

Among her many historical novels are *Jade* and *Lark*, which received wide critical acclaim. Miss Watson says that in doing her research for *Linnet*, "it was great fun to prowl around London and the Strand and Westminster, spotting all the places that Linnet and Colley and the rest went. . . ." In the lowest corridors of one of the Whitehall buildings where Westminster Palace once stood, the author discovered narrow lines of brass inlaid into the floor, marking the lines of the old palace— "perhaps the very spot where they were all ushered in to see Walsingham." Miss Watson also knows "the very spot where Giles lived in Guildford and the place on the London road where I'm sure Linnet chose to sit down on the bank and nurse her blistered heel."